D0622289

CRUCIBLE OF FOOLS

By the same author

Fiction:

HUNT FOR THE CLOWNS
THE KILLING OF YESTERDAY'S CHILDREN
LONELY THE MAN WITHOUT HEROES
A DARKNESS IN THE EYE
BRIDIE AND THE SILVER LADY
THE CRUCIFIXION OF SEPTIMUS ROACH

Non-fiction

SUMMER SOLDIER (with P. A. Williams)

CRUCIBLE OF FOOLS

M. S. POWER

HAMISH HAMILTON·LONDON

HAMISH HAMILTON LTD

Published by the Penguin Group
27 Wrights Lane, London W8 5TZ, England
Viking Penguin Inc., 40 West 23rd Street, New York, New York 10010, USA
Penguin Books Australia Ltd, Ringwood, Victoria, Australia
Penguin Books Canada Ltd, 2801 John Street, Markham, Ontario, Canada L3R 1B4
Penguin Books (NZ) Ltd, 182–190 Wairau Road Auckland 10, New Zealand

Penguin Books Ltd, Registered Offices: Harmondsworth, Middlesex, England

First published 1990
10 9 8 7 6 5 4 3 2 1

Filmset in Monophoto Baskerville
Printed in Great Britain by Butler and Tanner Ltd, Frome and London
A CIP catalogue record for this book is available from the British Library
ISBN 0–241–13006–9

For Richard and Patricia Brazier

with affection and gratitude

... and in their arrogance they saw nothing heinous in tormenting the demented, no sin in mocking the child closest to God. Yet they were the clowns, too stupid to recognize their wickedness, nurturing their intolerance in Ifreann, that crucible of fools.

The Visions and Visitations of Arthur Apple

BOOK ONE

I

The hills rose steeply either side of the narrow valley, and in one of them the river had its source. In winter they were bleak, the trees that clothed them leafless and standing erect and dark, sullen as reluctant guards, but in the spring when the buds glistened in the early dew and the gorse bloomed they were pretty enough, and the yellow flowers caught the weak sunlight and made the air seem warmer than it was.

The valley itself, however, was fertile and good to cultivate despite the fierce gales that hurtled unannounced down its length from the sea, bringing with them the smell of fish and the taste of salt, giving the inhabitants the odd quirk of constantly licking their lips.

The houses of the village of Ifreann, mostly one-storey, were built close together and in a straight line, hugging the base of the highest mountain, and throughout the year the heavy, blue-brown smoke from the peat fires hung low over the valley, hiding it from view. Some years earlier an enthusiastic council had begun to construct a road into the village but, for no explained reason, had abandoned the exercise, leaving it to stop abruptly some two miles from the outskirts. None of the villagers complained: it was, they felt, a sign from some friendly god that they were being protected from unwanted intrusion. Besides, the route the road would have taken came within a few yards of the perimeter of the graveyard, and it was wicked, wasn't it, to have traffic lumbering past, disturbing the untrammelled sleep of the dead?

*

It was remarkably still on the day of the funeral. Uncannily so. Some people nodded solemnly to each other as if they understood the reason for this and agreed that it was, really, a sign that it was the best thing that could have happened under the circumstances. Others shook their heads and wrung their hands and insisted it was a dreadful happening, wicked and unforgivable, something that would surely haunt them all for the rest of their natural lives. And some just shrugged their shoulders, dismissing the tragedy with cynical ease, too arrogant or too stupid to allow the death of an innocent man to impinge on their ordered existence.

Nevertheless, the whole village turned out to bury him, salving their consciences or merely curious; perhaps, in some cases, mouthing a prayer for the peaceful repose of his soul, perhaps just making certain that he was well and truly buried, his baleful gaze forever hidden by sods of heavy, damp earth. And there were flowers too – not many, but enough – mutely indicating that he had left behind in a few a guilty affection.

There is something extraordinary in the make-up of man that makes him shudder when confronted by gentleness in others, that makes the absence of malice accusatory. As though to negate this feeling he derides humility, equating it with weakness; and he scoffs at meekness, likening it to cowardice. In his arrogance he detects a fearful threat in anything that smacks of timidity, and he denounces it with mockery, using a buffoon's abuse to conceal his brutishness.

And so it was at the funeral. Even in death some of the men could not leave him in peace, strutting about as though at a market, each stride proclaiming that life belonged only to the aggressive. All the men stood well back from the graveside as though suspecting death might be contagious, and a group of six, clustered under the spindly, wind-swept cypresses, took to smoking, but

4

keeping their cigarettes cupped in their huge hands and out of sight of the priest whom they dreaded more than God Himself. One of them coughed and spat nicotine-stained mucus on to the ground, grinding it into the earth with the metallically reinforced toe of his boot. Noting this, his companions sniggered, finding something comically symbolic in the vulgar act.

When the ceremony was over, and the graveyard quiet and deserted, the rain came pelting down, making the new mound of reddish clay spatter over the flowers, flattening them, giving the petals the appearance of having been wounded, giving them, too, an appropriate appearance of death.

Within a week the earth had levelled itself and been grassed over with sods from under the hedge which surrounded the cemetery. The flowers had been removed, and there was no clue that Dan Loftus had ever existed.

2

'If you're waiting for me to die before getting married you'll be an old maid,' Mrs Ballerman told her daughter, settling herself into her comfortable chair by the kitchen range, shifting her bottom like a chicken on a clutch of eggs.

'Don't be silly, Mam,' Deirdre said. 'I'm waiting for no such thing and you know it. When I find the right man I'll marry him. I just haven't found him yet.'

'Your trouble is that you're too fussy, girl. A man is a man.'

'Not to me.'

'You can only have what's available.'

'Huh,' Deirdre snorted, and took her frustration out on the dough, kneading it vigorously, shaping it into an approximation of a male head and slamming it down on the marble surface, then pummelling it again.

'What's wrong with Peter Fox?' Mam wanted to know, merrily overlooking Peter's gross ugliness since she wouldn't have to bed him herself.

Deirdre gave her mother a withering glare.

'Well, Jimmy Stoddard then. He'd have you.'

'I'll find my own husband, thank you very much.'

It was Mam's turn to grunt. 'Huh,' she grunted. 'By the time you get round to making up your mind there won't *be* an unmarried man left in the village.'

'And who says I have to confine my choice to the village?' Deirdre demanded.

So it came as no great surprise when Deirdre Ballerman

married a man from the town fifteen miles away. She was always the rebellious one and a bit above herself, which was worse. Those huge black eyes of hers like polished coal would flash and strip the young men of their budding potency, turning them into floundering boys under her gaze, making them hugely awkward and fumbling despite their lewd, adolescent promises of what pleasures they would bestow on her if she would agree to step out with them.

'God,' Declan Burn would sigh, eyeing her grand big breasts. 'If only I could get my teeth into her.'

'It's not my teeth I want to get into her,' someone was sure to respond, and they'd all have a great laugh.

But wishing and longing was as far as any of them ever got, since Deirdre wouldn't give them the time of day. 'Grow up,' she'd snort. 'You have to know how to use what you've got, and what *you've* got wouldn't bring a smile to a pixie's face.'

However, Deirdre's choice of man flummoxed everyone. Dan Loftus was such a mild creature he had been given the reputation of being simple, and although this was unjustified it was understandable. He was forty-five, sixteen years older than Deirdre, tall and gangling and plain. It would never last, people prophesied gloomily but with sullen glee; and yet Deirdre clearly worshipped Dan, and that set everyone wondering as to what it was that he had about him that so mesmerised her.

'He's too old for you, girl,' Mam said wearily. 'He'll be dead long before you are, and then you'll end up like myself – alone and unwanted and haunted.'

'He's the man I want, Mam.'

'That's as may be, but what we want isn't always the best thing for us. And what you see in him I'll never understand. He's much too old, I tell you. You'll see. Mark my words.'

'He's *right* for me, Mam.'

7

'Right!' Mam scoffed. 'What would you know about right?'

'They're all saying you're too old for me, Dan.'
    'I am, probably.'
    It was a sunny, warm, dreamy afternoon, and they sat on the narrow outcrop of rocks holding hands, their bare feet dangling in the water. Out at sea, to their left, small fishing boats waddled in the swell; above them seagulls circled, silently, swallowing their raucous screams until the catch was hauled in. The scene was pretty as a picture.
    'Don't you be silly,' Deirdre said. 'Years have nothing to do with it.'
    'Not yet maybe.'
    'Don't you want me?'
    'Want you? Is it mad you've gone? More than anything in the world I want you.'
    'Honestly?'
    'Honestly.'
    'Mam says you'll die before I do and leave me alone.'
    'I might,' Dan told her sadly.
    'You won't, will you?'
    Dan smiled and squeezed her hand. 'I'll try not to.'
    'I know you will.'

It was a simple wedding with only Mrs Ballerman and her brother Tom – the politician as he was called, who came from the city for the occasion – as guests. Father Tierney married them, and he did it nicely although he sounded a bit sceptical from time to time as if he, too, didn't really expect them to make a go of it.
    After the ceremony Deirdre and her brand-new husband decided to walk home together along the dusty lanes, letting Mam and Tom go ahead in the trap, and they shaded their eyes as the pony's little feet threw up clouds of dust. In the hedgerow Dan spotted a clump of

8

late-flowering primroses: he bent and picked them, and presented them to Deirdre with exaggerated politeness, bowing a little. Later, Deirdre dried and pressed them, and kept them hidden in a small, lace-trimmed handkerchief, believing that if she were ever lonely she could peep at them and they would comfort her in the special way that only small, precious treasures can.

Mrs Ballerman had said that the only sensible thing for them to do was to move in with her. It would save them looking for a place of their own. It would save money too. And besides, she wouldn't be around for that much longer and then they'd have the place to themselves, and that was more than most people had in this day and age.

The house was a sturdy, two-storey, stone structure with mullioned windows which stood, isolated, on a narrow promontory that stuck out into the Atlantic like a jagged finger scolding foolhardy ships that plied the treacherous waters of the coast. Although the walls were very thick, it was a cold, damp house which wept summer and winter, and it was neglected since Mrs Ballerman refused to spend a penny on it: as long as the roof stayed on during the winter gales and there was enough glass in the windows to keep the flies out in the summer the house was sound to her way of thinking. That the rain seeped in at the eaves and tumbled into strategically placed plastic buckets through gaps in the slates was of no import. That the wallpaper was peeling (the once pink and yellow roses now a uniform dun) and the paintwork scabbed mattered not one whit. She spent her days and nights in the kitchen, sitting in the cushioned rocking chair by the range, or snoring on the iron bed in the corner farthest from the door. Her trips from the chair to the bed and back were all the exercise she took, and although she was no great age she liked to pretend she was, acting the crone and being bossy. 'Why?' she would demand when Deirdre

9

tried to change anything or clean the place up a bit. 'It's done us both all right until now and it'll do us both a bit longer.'

Mrs Ballerman liked to say that her heart had been broken, and perhaps it had. After only one year of marriage and three days after Deirdre was born her husband had drowned, and she had never quite abandoned the process of mourning. Dressed in black, a black lace bonnet skewered to her hair, she would rock herself back and forth in her chair and moan quietly to the faded sepia photograph of a burly young man with a wonderful curling moustache which stood in a silvered frame on the mantelshelf. And it was possibly this perpetuated grief that added twenty years to her appearance.

Mrs Ballerman welcomed Dan Loftus into her house with polite suspicion. She watched him a lot, of course, sometimes frowning, sometimes nodding to herself with what might have been approval, and she startled Deirdre one evening when they were alone by saying, 'It's high time you cleaned up this house a bit, and made it a decent home for a man to come back to when he's done working.'

'I thought –'

'Never mind what you thought, girl. You won't keep him another fortnight if he has to find his comfort somewhere else.'

Then, as if her sudden change of mind might be taken as a sign of weakness or generosity, she added, 'Although why you had to pick *him* I'll never understand. I still say he's too old for you, and that you'll end up living to regret it.'

And that night, as they got ready for bed, Deirdre took to studying Dan, looking for the tell-tale signs of approaching old age. She noted the grey tinges in the thinning hair and the slackness of the skin about his neck, and for a moment she wondered if her mother was right.

Then Dan got in beside her, and told her he loved her, and nothing else mattered.

'It's her own fault and no one else's for picking him,' the jealous young bucks said with smug satisfaction as the years passed and Deirdre produced no child. 'There's no juice in old prunes.'

'Bloody waste, fine woman like her.'

'Was.'

'Still is.'

'Better ones coming along.'

'Prettier maybe, but not as fine.'

Dan was the one who never gave up hope. 'We'll have a child. As soon as we're supposed to. As soon as it's right a child will come,' he said, trying the only way he knew to pacify Deirdre, who was close to desperation and had taken to weeping a lot when she thought no one could see her. Sometimes she would strip naked and stand in front of the long bevelled mirror in their bedroom, staring at her stomach, prodding it with her fingers, as if she might see or feel what was the cause of her infertility. And once she flew at old Mrs Ballerman, calling her nothing but an old witch, when she foolishly repeated her lament, 'I told you he was too old for you.'

'It's nothing to do with Dan,' Deirdre screamed. 'It's *me*.' Somehow she made that into an accusation of the old woman, but she meant it nevertheless. For some reason it never entered her thoughts that it might be Dan who was unable to procreate.

Then, miraculously, in the sixth year of their marriage, Deirdre found herself with child. She and Dan, hardly daring to believe it, joked about the inexplicable delay, creating absurd but hugely funny reasons for what might have hexed them. Cuddling up in bed, the blankets held tight to their chins, they giggled and whispered and became childlike in their joy.

But they waited two months before they told anyone, just in case it was a trick some impudent god was playing on them.

'You're sure?' Mrs Ballerman demanded.

Deirdre nodded. 'Yes, I'm sure. Quite sure.'

'And about time too,' her mother said. 'Keeping me here against my will,' she added mysteriously. 'I suppose you'll be able to cope?'

'Of course I will,' Deirdre told her, feeling that she could now cope with anything.

'Good. Good. Well, I can start getting ready then.'

'Ready? Ready for what, Mam?'

'Don't be silly, girl.'

'I'm not being silly. Ready for what?'

Mrs Ballerman gave her an odd but friendly look, and said nothing.

There was great dignity in the way Mrs Ballerman arranged herself to die. Oddly, as she readied herself, she seemed sturdier and younger and more content. All day Friday she put her papers in order, tearing up old letters and burning them in the range that had warmed her body just as the letters had once warmed her spirit; and it was curious that as the pages caught fire and turned in upon themselves, so too Mrs Ballerman seemed to withdraw pleasurably into herself, folding her soul, packaging it nicely for the journey.

She spent hours emptying boxes – little ones, made of flower-printed cardboard and tied with ribbons to match the flowers – and burning the contents of these also, secretively, watching intently as the flames consumed them, with a wistful smile of satisfaction on her crinkled face. Being practical, she kept the boxes, putting them back in the bottom drawer of the chest, in case they proved useful to someone else.

'What on earth are you doing, Mam?' Deirdre asked.

'Getting ready,' Mam said tritely.

'You keep saying that. Ready for what, in heaven's name?'

Mrs Ballerman gave her daughter that look again.

One afternoon she asked Dan to be so kind as to carry her bed upstairs to what had been the bedroom she had shared with her husband, dismissing protestations about the cold and damp and dreariness of that unused room by ignoring them and repeating her request.

When Dan came downstairs again she asked, 'All set up?'

'All set up,' Dan told her.

'Good.'

Mrs Ballerman heaved herself out of her chair and plumped up the cushions, patting them affectionately as if they were friendly, furry creatures. She glanced about the kitchen in the manner of someone checking to make sure they'd forgotten nothing. Then she released her hair from the net which had restrained it in a bun for so many years, and shook her head youthfully. Carefully she burned the net. She took the photograph of her husband from the mantelshelf, said goodnight, and retired, taking her time about climbing the stairs, saying, 'Up we go,' to the photograph, and smiling.

On Sunday morning, early and without a murmur, she died, looking very pleased with herself and with the way things had gone, clutching the framed photograph in both hands.

3

Despite the lingering sadness of Mam's passing, Deirdre's was a wondrous, mystical pregnancy. Full-wombed and gloriously happy, she strode to the village each and every day, flaunting her triumph, visiting the small shop to buy groceries, many of which she did not need nor want. Her dark eyes flashed at anyone who looked at her, and taunted, 'What have you to say now?' And as though to justify their pessimism old women would shake their heads and mutter, 'She's left it too late, of course. It'll never be healthy and probably won't live all that long,' enjoying their gloominess.

A great contentment overwhelmed Deirdre. Nothing pleased her more than to stand at the window and watch her dear Dan working in the fields, and stroke her belly, crooning to the new life within her, recalling gentle lullabies or making up her own words to old melodies when the original ones escaped her. Sometimes she didn't even bother with words, using the tune to soothe herself and the kicking child, and in her mind's eye she saw the infant gurgle and snuggle down peacefully on the cushions of her womb.

At night she and Dan would count the weeks, he with his cheek pressed to her swollen belly pretending he could hear the child whisper secrets to him, and teasing Deirdre by refusing to divulge those secrets; while she, running her fingers through Dan's thinning grey hair, would tell him what a silly he was, or pretend to pout at being excluded from such intimacy.

*

'It's not healthy just to sit with my feet up, Dan. The books say I should take exercise, and that's what I'm going to do.'

'Well, just see to it that you don't overdo things, that's all.'

'I won't. Don't fuss so. You're like a broody hen, I swear.'

'Hah. Well, just be careful.'

'Of course I'll be careful, silly.'

'And leave all the heavy work to me.'

'I promise I'll only do as much as I feel able to.'

Thus Deirdre spent her days cleaning and painting the house, but taking her time about it, resting every now and then, and being careful as she climbed the small stepladder. What she enjoyed most about all this activity was that she wasn't alone: she talked aloud all the while to the unborn child within her, saying, 'That's better, isn't it?' Or, standing back to admire the once shabby wall, now glowing with bright, warm magnolia paint, 'Now, that's prettier, don't you think, my precious?' Or, having scrubbed the hall until the flagstones shone like polished gun-metal, 'Surely, you could eat your breakfast off that now, couldn't you?' And she would remonstrate good-naturedly with Dan if he neglected to wipe his boots thoroughly on the mat by the door and carried globs of soil into the house so spick and span.

And when she rested in her work to have a cup of tea she would test the tea before drinking, making sure it wasn't too hot so that the child could share it with her, and she would take only small sips, so as not to overtax the little throat.

Dan worked hard on the farm. Over the years he had greatly improved the condition of the soil and upgraded the stock; now he was more concerned about the look of the place. First impressions are important, he told himself, and it became his small obsession that the farm should look beautiful when the child first set eyes on it. So he laid all the hedges and trimmed them neatly and bound the twisted branches with twisted hemp, bidding them stay in place. He rebuilt those sections of the walls that had tumbled, structuring them like lace so that the wind could blow through them and not buffet them causing them to collapse again. He got new slates for the cowshed and whitewashed it inside and out, muttering dark warnings to the cattle as they swished their tails and wrote their graffiti with dung. He rewired the window of the chicken house because it looked a bit rusty, and borrowed Deirdre's scrubbing brush to scour the laying boxes. He even sold off the flock of Rhode Island Reds and replaced them with Leghorns, since he felt that their whiteness looked prettier, their fiery combs more decorative.

He was inexplicably filled with a sense of continuity, and as he worked he envisioned generations of Loftuses doing the same chores he was doing, they for their children as he for his, and this made him happier than he had ever been.

In the evenings Dan and Deirdre sat together in silence either side of the range, listening to the crackle of burning wood, the curious song of the night wind and the occasional contented lowing of the cattle in the byre next door, admiring the new curtains and chair covers which Deirdre had made, and which the moon, reflecting from the sea, made shimmer in the same way the material had shimmered on the glossy page of the catalogue.

On one such evening towards the end of September, out of the blue, as Dan stretched out a bootless foot and tickled Deirdre's shin with his toe, Deirdre announced, 'I'd like to call him Sergei.'

Nonplussed, 'That's Russian,' Dan said, unable to think of anything better to say.

'I know. but it's such a beautiful name, isn't it?'

Dan chuckled.

'Don't you like it?'

'If you like it that's all that counts.' Then a thought struck him, and he chuckled again. 'It might not be a boy. What will you do then?'

'Oh, it's a boy all right. Have no fear on that score. It's a boy for sure and no mistaking it.'

There was a calendar advertising Craven A cigarettes hanging by the door of the kitchen, and they took it in turns to strike off the days to the birth as they went upstairs to bed, using the pencil tied to the door hinge for just that purpose. And as each day was struck off, they kissed each other and smiled with their eyes.

4

It was a difficult, pain-filled, prolonged birth. For five hours Mrs Farrell, the midwife, toiled. Dan, who had been told to keep out of the way, paced the kitchen in a daze and wished Mrs Farrell would call for more hot water since that distracted him and took his mind off the terrible possibilities which swarmed in his mind and terrified him.

Mrs Farrell's youngest son sat at the table chewing on an enormous hunk of bread smeared with dripping. For an eight-year-old he was remarkably nonchalant about the whole affair, but he was always dragged along when his mother was called out, 'just in case', and he was used to it. It was he who was sent skittering off for the doctor when Mrs Farrell finally admitted that she could not cope.

While he was away Mrs Farrell said, 'Why don't you sit yourself down, Dan, and I'll make us both a cup of tea,' calling him Dan since she felt the familiarity was comforting and motherly and just what a man needed at a time like this.

Dan sat as he was told and accepted the tea, but he didn't drink it. He stared at the liquid and thought it was too dark and nothing like the way Deirdre made it. Then it struck him that maybe she'd never make tea for him again, and a low moan escaped him which Mrs Farrell took as a sigh of returning contentment. 'There,' she said. 'I told you you'd feel better after a cup of tea. There's nothing like a good cup of tea in times of stress. Better than all the medicines in the world,' she added, sipping her own noisily as if noise enhanced its flavour.

Alone upstairs Deirdre, bathed in sweat and close to panic, was blaming herself for all the difficulty. She tossed her head about and made rash promises to God if He would only see to it that everything turned out all right. When she heard the iron shoes of the doctor's pony knocking sparks from the cobbles of the yard, and the rattle of the trap wheels, she took it as a sign that a deal had been struck with God, that He had taken her up on her promises, and for a while she fretted since she could not now recall all the bargains she had made. In an attempt to distract herself she tried to eavesdrop on what the voices downstairs were saying, but quickly abandoned this exercise when all she could distinguish was a low murmuring which could have been God Himself complaining that she had reneged on the deal.

'Believe me,' Dr McCann told Dan, accepting the tumbler of whiskey and downing it in one gulp. 'Believe me, there's not a thing in the world for you to worry about. She's a fine strong woman that wife of yours and she'll be right as rain in no time. In no time,' he repeated thrusting his tumbler forward.

'And the boy?'

'Didn't you hear the howls of him? Grand. Grand. Lungs like a Caruso in him. And the size of him! Small wonder we had a job getting him into the world in one piece.'

Dan nodded, and grinned sheepishly. He had, indeed, heard the howls and had felt an emotion swelling within him the like of which he had never before experienced. He wanted to rush upstairs and grab the child and take him far from all the pain and hurt and bewilderment, take him out into the fields and just sit there with him, telling him that everything was all right now, that his father was there to look after him and protect him, that he'd never have to suffer for another minute of his life. But he hadn't done that. He had remained hunched in a chair, shaking, as close to tears as he'd ever been, learning the full meaning of helplessness.

It wasn't until well after the doctor had gone, and Mrs Farrell had finished telling him to make sure he put the baby the right way up in the crib (all the while clamping her hat – a monstrous affair like a fedora but decorated with a brace of balding pigeons – on her head) and closed the door behind her that he climbed the stairs, hauling himself up by the handrail, and peeped timidly into the bedroom.

Only a small lamp was lit, and it threw a golden light on the bed, illuminating a scene that took his breath away. Deirdre looked as though she was asleep. The child, so small, so fragile, nuzzled her breast and sucked hungrily. It was the most beautiful thing Dan had ever seen. He crept in and sat gingerly on the edge of the bed, staring wide-eyed at them. Deirdre opened her eyes and smiled at him; then she closed her eyes again, and Dan reached out to touch her. But he changed his mind and folded his arms and just sat there, wondering what it was that he had noticed in her eyes.

It seemed an interminable time before the baby stopped feeding: a brittle dawn was streaking the sky with crimson, and the first birds had started their shivering songs. Gently Dan took the baby and carried him to the wooden crib, setting him down gently and covering him with the woolly blankets Deirdre had chosen from the catalogue along with the curtain material. Then, straightening, Dan stood there, staring at the boy, looking almost bewildered, shaking his head from time to time and sighing twice.

'I'm sorry,' Deirdre whispered in a tiny voice.

'Sorry? Sorry for what, in heaven's name?'

But Deirdre didn't reply. She turned her face away and closed her eyes again, and Dan supposed her strange

20

apology had something to do with her being distraught and confused.

That evening and all through the night it snowed, and Dan decided that this was a good omen. All the earth's blemishes were concealed under the snow, and everything looked clean and bright and pure.

Three days after his birth the child was baptised. Deirdre would have liked her uncle Tom to have been godfather but he had shingles again. So they asked Mrs Farrell and Dr McCann to be godparents, and Father Tierney performed the ceremony with aplomb, not batting an eyelid when he christened the boy Sergei Daniel.

'You'll be calling him Dan like yourself,' he said to Dan quietly, pocketing the christening fee thankfully.

Dan glanced at Deirdre, who was already moving down the path. He shrugged his eyebrows and clamped his hat firmly on his head. 'I think not,' he said.

5

In the year of Sergei's second birthday, spring took its time about coming. The sea clung to its skin of Damascus steel until the last week of May. The small, less robust birds jabbered shrilly in tones of dismay, arguing about what had become of the times as the cold winds blew them helter-skelter along the coast, exhausting them and making them peevish and irritable. The trees, deformed by generations of gales, outlined starkly against the wet grey sky, took on the appearance of old, bent women, their backs to the ocean, bracing themselves against the buffeting chill. Old people urged their spirits to make an extra effort to surmount the prolonged inclemency and took to whispering to themselves as if by doing so they could distract whatever demon might be sent to whisk them away.

Then, overnight, spectacularly, everything changed: the sea stopped its heaving and dyed itself duck-egg blue, great sumptuous buds appeared on the trees, primroses spattered the hedgerow with pale yellow, and rooks scavenged noisily for twigs, working overtime.

In the village windows were thrown open, and the old people slept better now that their critical time of year seemed to have passed. The winter tightness of their faces relaxed as they optimistically set out to deal with what was left of the year, and they took their time over their prayers as if they were less urgently needed.

Dan was the first to admit – but only to himself – that

there was something amiss with his son. Oddly, he felt no sadness, no surging compassion. He spent longer and longer in the fields, consumed by a terrible anger, and as he ploughed and planted he raged aloud, sometimes blinding himself as he used his fists brutally to scrub away his tears of utter fury. At first he blamed himself, then God, then that oblique thing called Fate for lumbering his son with a dullness of mind, but he was too honest and generous to sustain these unjust accusations for long.

One day, with the long, stinging rods of spring rain pelting down on him, he yanked hard on the slippery leather reins and pulled the steaming horses to a halt. He secured the reins to the shaft of the plough and stood perfectly still for several minutes, as though petrified. Then, slowly at first but building into a frenzy, he beat himself about the head with both clenched fists and roared, 'That's enough,' and from that moment he set about making the best of the crippling with which the Almighty had chosen to afflict them.

'They said it was too early to be certain, but they said it in a way that didn't seem to hold out much hope,' Dan said.

They were sitting by the iron range, as they did every evening after Sergei had been put to bed. The warmth of the days seemed to make dusk that much colder, and the fret from the sea got into the bones and stiffened them if they weren't coddled a little. In unspoken agreement Deirdre had requisitioned her mother's rocker, and Dan, opposite, sat in a new wing-backed chair, a 'man's' chair he had purchased with some vague idea about its being passed on through generations. He liked to imagine its being spoken about and him with it: 'It was old Dan Loftus who bought this, you know – what a character *he* was!', he would hear people say in his mind, creating them to his liking and seeing them quite clearly.

Deirdre ignored Dan's statement. She pretended not to have heard it, and stealthily withdrew her mind from the possibility of irresolvable sadness, rocking back and forth.

'Did you hear me?' Dan asked.

Deirdre made no reply. She leaned forward and prodded the logs in the range, rattling the poker against the bars as though to obliterate all other sound. One of the logs sparked with a sound like rifle-fire, making her jump, and she dropped the poker on the hearth. She left it there, settling back in her chair, rocking again.

'We're going to have to face up to it,' Dan said aloud but meaning to speak only to himself.

Deirdre wasn't about to face up to anything. Since the moment of his birth she had shown a wariness towards her son, longing to show him affection but unable to. It was as though she had known instantly that something was wrong and had blamed herself for that blemish. She felt cheated. More, she believed she was being punished for some wrong she had done but that the precise nature of that wrong was being maliciously concealed from her. Certainly, she fed and tended the boy, allowing him his fill and keeping him spotless, but her care was perfunctory. She began to have long periods of brooding, and it was common for her to be morose. Her famed fiery temper sparked only occasionally and even when it did it had little potency, a damped-down version of its original self, and after each outburst she would spend many days in total silence as though doing penance.

She seldom ventured outside the house now, certainly never farther than the small garden Dan had created for her, planting it with herbs and rich-coloured cottage plants. She spent long hours in a kind of trance, standing by the window, her arms folded, gazing out, a curious wistfulness in her eyes. Or she would sit in the rocking chair, the curve of the chair contorting her body into the

lines of old age, staring at Sergei as he played with the
blocks of wood Dan had fashioned into fascinating shapes
and painted the colours of the rainbow, thinking that
perhaps it was true what the old crones whispered: that
she had transmitted all her obstinacy and wilfulness to
him, and she would shudder when she spotted in his eyes
the angry fire that had once been in hers. Yet she could
see there was a gentleness about the child too, and that
pleased her and eased her pain; she knew that part of him
would have come from Dan, and something told her it
was important to have this link between them.

Once she had taken Sergei on her knee and read to him
pretty, happy-ever-after stories from a thin little book
which some long forgotten aunt had given her at about
Sergei's age, but as the child's head lolled about and his
eyes remained blank and stupid she had put him back on
the floor and ripped the book to shreds as though it
contained blasphemies of a most horrific nature.

Dan salvaged the little book, putting it back together
again, carefully sticking in the tattered pages and rein-
forcing the cover with pieces of thick cardboard. The work
done, he placed the book on a high shelf with other items
he had rescued from Deirdre's tantrums, telling himself
they would all be there, ready to come down and be used
again, when Deirdre got over her trouble.

And thus, with Dan working away on the farm, content,
as he thought of it, to allow Deirdre to recover herself in
her own time; and Deirdre retreating ever further into
the woeful world of confusion and resentment she daily
created; and Sergei growing physically strong and sturdy
and handsome while his mind remained dim and
unstirred, five years passed. At the end of that time it was
decided by those who know about such things that there
was still nothing that could be done for the boy.

The specialist was sympathetic, but he had a nervous

habit of glancing at the clock on the wall of his consulting room which was off-putting and made one feel one was wasting the great man's time. 'It's just one of those unfathomable things, I'm afraid,' he told Dan, experience having taught him that it worked better to make things unfathomable than to try to explain the intricacies of mental deficiency to 'the people'. 'And there's really not another thing I can tell you,' he added, aware that by professing bafflement of his own he would alleviate the confusion of the man who sat opposite him, staring blankly across the desk. As a city man, he felt he should tell Dan to have faith since it struck him as fair medical practice, under the circumstances, to encourage the peasantry by administering a drop of the occult as no pills or lotions would be forthcoming. However, something about Dan's eyes made him change his mind, and he said instead, 'I can only say that there's nothing really for you to worry about. The boy is slow, of course, but that is no reason for him not leading a wholesome, normal life, is it?' He heaved a short sigh by way of pooh-poohing any such notion. 'You understand?' he asked, and then frowned as if puzzled by his own question. Dan, however, nodded.

The doctor brightened. 'And who can tell? Perhaps with patience and understanding he will improve. I've known it happen.' Dan nodded again.

'Time alone will tell,' the specialist predicted, standing and holding out his hand, and repeating this philosophy he guided Dan to the door. 'Time alone will tell,' he repeated, sounding like a man who had waited all his life for time to tell him something.

Later, when he thought about it, he remembered it had come like one of those extraordinary flashes you read about in the Bible. Dan was hosing down the cowshed. It was a chore he enjoyed and did fastidiously. There was something about sending the fierce jet of water up on to the walls and into the rafters and watching it tumble back, coloured by the sunlight, that satisfied him. Sergei liked it too: sitting in his special place (a sort of throne made from bales of straw) he clapped his hands and beamed. 'Look Sergei!' Dan told him, 'look at the colours', and Sergei looked and saw the colours and clapped some more.

Suddenly, Dan stopped hosing, letting the nozzle fall into the hole which drew the water from the byre, and gazed solemnly at his son. Then, with great deliberation, he switched off the water at the tap and started to coil the hose around the two huge nails he had embedded in the wall near the door. He wiped his hands on his overalls and hoisted Sergei on to his shoulders, a leg either side of his head. Then he jog-trotted to the house, and into the kitchen, trailing mud along the floor but ignoring it.

Deirdre was at the sink, peeling potatoes, taking her time about it, trying to keep the skin from each potato in one piece, She had succeeded with three or four and these lay curling prettily on the draining board. She looked up briefly as Dan came in, her face expressionless.

'It's time we started the boy at school,' Dan announced, swinging Sergei from his perch and placing him gently on the floor. The boy's legs folded beneath him and he squatted, looking as if he was about to cry but, distracted, he took to following the design in the rug with his finger. The smile which had optimistically planted itself on Dan's face slowly disintegrated. 'What do you think?' he asked.

For quite some time Deirdre made no reply. She continued to peel the vegetables methodically. She could have been thinking, but Dan knew that wasn't the case: she was, he knew, trying to dismiss the question from her mind. She was saying to herself if I ignore it it will go away; it will be like it was.

'Did you hear me?'

'I heard you.'

'Well?'

27

Deirdre put down the peeler and washed her hands under the tap. Then she turned and faced Dan, not giving Sergei a glance. 'There's no point, and you know it,' she said flatly.

Dan was shocked. 'What d'you mean, no point? Of course there's a point. He might not understand everything but he'll learn something. Anyway, it's high time he started to meet boys his own age.'

'No,' Deirdre said.

'You're being unreasonable.'

Deirdre didn't answer that for a while. She went to the window and stared out, shaking herself gently. Then she turned and gazed at Sergei playing on the rug. Finally, very quietly, with something like menace in her voice, she said, 'No one's going to have Sergei. He's never going to be taken away from me. Never.'

That evening, after she had put Sergei to bed, Deirdre didn't come down. She went straight to bed, leaving Dan to sit by the range by himself for the first time since they had wed.

A week later, at midday, when Dan came to the house for a bite of food, Deirdre rounded on him. 'You've been to the school, haven't you?' she snapped. 'And behind my back.'

Dan sat down at the table, taking his time. 'I went to the school, yes. I wanted to see what they could do for Sergei. It wasn't behind your back.'

'I told you I won't let anyone take him away.'

'Nobody's trying to take him away, Deirdre. He'll just go to classes in the morning and be home in the afternoon.

'No,' Deirdre said.

'The teacher thinks he should,' Dan tried.

'I know. She was here this morning.'

'Oh. And?'

'And nothing. I told her to leave us alone.'

28

'Deirdre, the boy needs some schooling.'

'We'll give him all the schooling he needs.'

'We can't.'

'Oh dear,' was what Dr McCann said to Dan. 'Well, of course, she's *bound* to be somewhat depressed. It's very difficult for a woman, you know, to understand why she has produced a child who isn't – who isn't – well ... who is a bit slow.' He coughed, and looked away, and rubbed the side of his nose.

'She's always brooding now,' Dan explained. 'And getting worse.'

And that was certainly true. Deirdre spoke hardly at all, except to herself and sometimes, when she thought she was alone, to her dead mother. And once when Dan came back to the house unexpectedly, he was shocked to find her dressed in her mother's clothes, standing in front of the mirror in the hall, laughing in crazed spurts. Somehow Dan realised that she had no idea what she was laughing at, and when she spotted Dan watching her she stopped her wild giggling and frowned as if trying to think who he was. Then she spun around and went upstairs, and Dan heard her weeping pitifully.

'I can give you some tablets for her,' Dr McCann said.

'She'd never take them.'

'You couldn't persuade her?'

Dan shook his head.

'Maybe I – ' the doctor began.

Dan shook his head again. 'She'd kill me if she knew I'd said anything to you.'

'Perhaps hospital – '

'Oh no,' Dan said. 'Not a hospital. That would be the end of her for sure.'

'Well, there isn't really anything else I can suggest.'

'Maybe it will wear off,' Dan suggested hopefully, and hopefully too Dr McCann clasped at that possibility, and said, 'Yes, maybe. You never can tell with these things, you know. The mind is a funny thing,' he concluded, even smiling as if indeed the mind was amusing.

6

Autumn came, crisp and white and starched as an apron. And with its coming Deirdre seemed to improve a little. She busied herself, bustling about the house cleaning, or spending long hours in the kitchen by the stove preparing fruits and vegetables for bottling, hoarding as energetically as a squirrel. Dan wrote the labels for the bottles, pleased to be involved: PLUMS, ONIONS, WALNUTS, he wrote, printing the words and going over the names several times to make his writing thicker, BEETROOT, CARROTS, RADISH. In the pantry off the kitchen the potatoes had been piled in their bed of straw, and beside them the root crops too large for pickling: white turnips, swedes, mangels. Above these, hanging from the rafters, the joints of gammon Dan had smoked in the shed by the byre, wrapped in muslin.

'Well, one thing is sure – we won't starve this winter,' Dan observed one evening.

'No,' Deirdre replied, her voice vague.

Dan rose from the table and stretched. 'We're luckier than most,' he said.

'Yes,' said Deirdre, sprinkling salt on the concoction she was mixing.

'I like the autumn,' Dan said suddenly.

'Do you,' Deirdre replied, making a statement rather than asking a question.

'Yes,' Dan told her. 'I really do. It's as if the earth was getting ready for bed after a right good day's work. You know, really tired but satisfied too.'

Deirdre stopped stirring her mixture and balanced the wooden spoon on the edge of the big pot. She wiped her hands in her apron, and as an afterthought wiped her brow too. Through the apron she said something which Dan didn't catch.

'Hmm?' he asked.

'Nothing.'

'Tell me.'

'It was nothing.'

And: 'It's nothing,' Dr McCann said. 'Just a bit of a cold. A day in bed, kept warm, will see him right as rain.'

But Sergei's bit of a cold developed into something more serious, and within a week he had been taken to the hospital, his little body glistening with perspiration, wrapped in a blanket and a feathery eiderdown.

'You said it was nothing,' Deirdre shrieked at Dr McCann.

'Hush,' said Dan.

'I won't hush. He said it was nothing. He said it on purpose. He wants Sergei to die.'

'My dear Mrs Loftus –' Dr McCann began.

'Don't you Mrs Loftus me,' Deirdre shouted.

'Hush, Deirdre,' Dan tried again.

'I won't hush,' Deirdre repeated.

'There is no question of your son dying, Mrs Loftus,' Dr McCann pointed out. 'He is ill, certainly, but in a week or two he'll be home as healthy and hale as ever he was.'

'You see?' Dan said, putting a comforting arm about his wife's shoulder, shaking her a little, and adding, 'Silly old thing, making such a fuss.'

Four days later, at seven minutes past three in the morning, Sergei died. He died alone since no one was expecting him to go, and in death his little blue eyes showed an intelligence and a peace they had never contained in life.

It was an awful funeral. Only women attended but they brought their children out of respect for the dead boy's age. It didn't rain, but the sky glowered and was hostile. The women seemed at a loss as to what to say, their stock phrase, 'Sure, he had a good life,' being untrue. Perhaps that was why some of them just nudged each other and pointed by nodding their black-hatted heads at Dan and Deirdre, who stood apart, not comforting each other as would be expected.

It was the first time I'd seen Dan close-up. Mam had me by the hand and was saying to him how sorry she was. He thanked her, then settled his eyes on me. He just kept looking and looking at me. I smiled and he smiled back, and there was something in his smile that made me certain we were friends.

'A fine boy,' Dan said to Mam.

Mam looked down at me. 'Yes. Yes. That he is.'

Dan reached out as though to tousle my hair, but he saw Deirdre eyeing him curiously so he withdrew his hand and gave me another smile.

'He's a nice man, isn't he, Mam?' I asked later.

'Who, dear?'

'Mr Loftus.'

'Is that 'cause he said you were a fine boy?' Mam asked, teasing.

'No.'

'I'm only teasing you. Yes, he's a nice man. God knows he'll need to be now. Need all the patience in the world, I shouldn't wonder.'

That was Mam's way of solving all problems, to invoke the virtue of patience. Like the wives of all fishermen, she had practised it diligently. It wasn't a passive, tolerant patience though. There was an odd fury about it as though

God, Who controlled the lives of men and the elements they battled against, had to be kept up to His job.

'I'm just nipping down to wait for your Dad,' Mam would say, tucking me up in bed, making sure the old eiderdown covered my feet, and planting a quick kiss on my forehead. And I'd say, 'Wrap yourself up well, Mam,' and she'd give me one of her little smiles that said how pleased she was I was looking after her so well. 'And be sure to wake me up when you get back.'

'I'll do that.'

She never did wake me though, and for some reason I never once asked her why. Except the night Dad didn't come back. That night she woke me.

One night I followed her, keeping well back, with my eyes fixed on the oil lantern she carried. She swung it as though she was singing and using the lantern to keep the beat, and I found myself trying to find a tune to fit in with hers.

On the cliff top she joined half a dozen other women, huddled together against the cold, woollen shawls over their heads, protecting their ears from the wicked, biting wind. They didn't talk much, just the odd word, it seemed. They stared out into the darkness of the sea, scanning the blackness for a sign of the green-white glow that heralded the incoming boats, and sometimes cocking their heads, and saying, 'Hush a minute,' thinking they could hear something. And when they saw the lights or heard the sound, they embraced each other, and rejoiced, and ran like schoolgirls down the path to the harbour.

You know how it is when you wake up with a start, knowing something is wrong but with no idea what it is? Well, that's how it was. It might have been because only one set of footsteps came up the path instead of two. Or it might have been Mam's grief somehow transmitting itself to me in my sleep. Anyway, I was awake in a flash, and knowing something was wrong.

'Mam?' I called. 'Mam?'

Mam didn't answer. She came up the stairs very slowly and I could hear her giving little sniffs, trying to compose herself before she got to my room. Typically she said, 'You should be asleep.'

'I just woke up.'

'Oh.'

'What's the matter, Mam?' I asked.

'Shush a while,' said Mam, so I knew then that it was serious, since telling me to shush was her way of gaining time to gather her thoughts. She'd said shush, too, before she told me that she'd lost the baby she'd been carrying for seven months; and shush, too, when the thatch on Auntie Bridie's house caught fire and burnt her to death. So, I just lay there, watching her, waiting for her to tell me the bad news.

And eventually she did tell me that Dad had been lost. She said, 'I'll be back,' and went to her room, coming back in her nightdress and getting into bed beside me. She cuddled me very close, her cheek against mine, her eyelashes fluttering against my skin like butterflies. And once she'd told me I could feel her tears running down my face, warm and gentle and all the sadder for that.

'There's just the two of us now,' she said. 'Just the two of us. And you the man of the house.'

'I'll look after you, Mam.'

'I know you will.'

And when I got home from school Mam was dressed all in black, and Dad's clothes had all been packed, wrapped in parcels of thick brown paper and tied with string, and the house had been scrubbed from top to bottom, and all she'd kept was a single photograph of Dad, showing him as a young man. But even if you hadn't

35

known him, something about that photograph told you it was the image of someone dead.

7

Without Sergei the farmhouse seemed to take on a strange coldness, as if the stones from which it was built also felt the chill of grief, and retained it. Even the range seemed to give out less heart, something Dan would have put down to morbid imagination were it not that the kettle certainly took several minutes longer to boil. In tacit, unspoken agreement neither he nor Deirdre spoke about the dead child. Indeed, they hardly spoke at all, and their silence made the house that much gloomier. Not that there was anger or bitterness between them: there simply seemed to be nothing to say.

Deirdre moved about the house in silence, faithfully doing the chores. She didn't hum to herself now, nor sing. She even seemed to walk in silence, her footsteps making no sound. Her eyes became dull, and the skin beneath them turned black-blue and stayed that way. And there was a sagging of her shoulders which aged her greatly.

Dan, on the other hand, out in the fields, ranted furiously to himself, cursing the plough and the earth and the stones that impeded his way. But it was impotent cursing since he no longer felt an affection for the soil. His interest seemed to have died with his son, and when he himself died the farm would pass into the hands of strangers, so there was little point in cosseting it, making it a jewel to leave his offspring.

'Are you coping?' Dr McCann wanted to know, making

it clear that he just happened to be in the neighbourhood and thought he'd look in.

'Yes,' Dan told him.

'Good,' Dr McCann said, nodding, relieved. 'And Mrs Loftus?'

Dan shrugged.

'Ah,' Dr McCann sighed. 'You should see to it that she gets out more, you know.'

Dan nodded.

'Not good for a woman to stay cooped up with sorrow.'

'No.'

'Perhaps I should look in – ?' Dr McCann suggested, leaving the question hanging.

Dan shook his head. 'I wouldn't, I think.'

'No?'

'No.'

'Oh. Well. Perhaps you're right. I'll be off then. If you need me, you know where I am.'

'Yes.'

Dan watched the doctor drive away, flapping the reins on the pony's back and clicking with his tongue.

Two weeks after Sergei had been buried (close enough to his grandmother but in the plot set aside for children because of some vague belief that the souls of dead children might like to play together), Deirdre did something strange. She moved all her belongings into the room where her mother had died, made up the bed and took to sleeping there on her own. Oddly, Dan didn't mind. It made his loneliness complete, and that, he felt, was how loneliness should be. Besides, lying there in the dark with only a whiff of Deirdre's perfume for company, he was able, sometimes, to remember how things used to be, and there was contentment enough in that.

The first snow of the winter fell on the third of December.

Huge, glistening flakes tumbled down, and in no time the countryside was white and smooth and bright. The trees on the mountainside groaned under the unaccustomed weight, and an old stag trumpeted warnings of possible hunger to follow.

In the kitchen, Dan stirred his black, sweet tea and watched Deirdre from the corner of his eye. She seemed different that morning: jerky in her actions and wringing her hands a lot. She kept touching her hair, patting it as if she felt it was continually falling out of place. Suddenly she came to the table and sat opposite Dan. 'I was talking to Sergei last night,' she said in a quiet, matter-of-fact voice.

Dan nodded.

'He wants to see me.'

Dan nodded again. There was nothing new in this. Deirdre often 'talked' to the dead boy, finding communication with him easier now that he was dead.

'You don't believe me.'

'I believe you, Deirdre,' Dan told her, and he meant it. Indeed, he too had gone through strange little experiences, once imagining he had seen Sergei sitting on the gate, waiting for him to come in from the field, waiting to be hoisted on his shoulders and carried, laughing in his curious way, into the house. Dan had set off at a trot towards the gate, stopping only when the vision dissolved, leaving him stunned and weeping.

The snow ceased falling around midday, and a cold, brittle sun came out. Carrying pitchfork loads of silage into the byre in readiness for the milking, Dan took a breather, removing his heavy oilskin and stretching. As he stretched, he sensed something was wrong. He frowned and squinted and scratched an armpit, and had almost convinced himself he was imagining things when he noticed there was no smoke rising from the chimney. Now that's odd, he thought, and, worried that the range might have gone out and Deirdre be cold, he made his way, without haste, to the house.

The kitchen was empty, the house very quiet, the fire in the range indeed out. 'Deirdre,' he called. 'Deirdre?' There was no answer. He went upstairs, tip-toeing in case she was asleep. She was not in her bedroom. He tried his room and the bathroom. Then he went downstairs again, taking the stairs two at a time. He stood in the kitchen, shaking his head: surely she hadn't gone out on a day like this? He shivered as a sudden cold draught crossed the kitchen, making the door to the pantry creak open an inch. Something about the tiny movement petrified Dan; for several moments he stood, staring at the door. Then he moved across the kitchen and pushed the pantry door wide open.

Deirdre was hanging from one of the hooks, her body still swinging between the hams, her face blue, her tongue protruding from her mouth as though life had been whipped from her as she licked her lips.

Oddly, Dan felt nothing. Those fragile membranes of the mind that ensure sanity snapped, but Dan didn't know it. He was never to know it. Only the villagers were aware that Dan Loftus had suddenly gone mad.

'Is it true what they say about Mr Loftus, Mam?'
  'What do they say?'
  'That he's gone cracked.'
  Mam winced. 'You shouldn't listen to such talk.'
  'I can't help hearing it when they tell me, Mam.'
  'You shouldn't listen,' Mam said unreasonably.
  'Is it true?'
  'He's – not well.'
  'Oh. He *is* mad.'
  'Maybe.'
  'He'll be all right though, won't he?'
  'Of course he will. God will look after him.'

'Oh,' I said again, not feeling all that reassured. Despite Mam's rigorous faith in God, I wasn't so sure. God, to my way of thinking, had the queerest way of looking after people and things, and I can't say I was too happy about leaving Mr Loftus's fate in His hands. After all, He hadn't exactly repaid Mam's love for Him – it struck me as a pretty one-sided affair.

'– God looks after everyone in trouble,' Mam was saying.

'Oh. That's fine then,' I said.

'Yes. Yes it is,' Mam insisted, and took to pounding the washing so that suds spattered everywhere, making her tut, and say, 'Now look at what you made me do!'

I nearly said that if God looked after those who were in trouble He'd surely have fixed things so she didn't have to take in other people's washing, but I didn't. I knew she hated doing it, but as she always told me, 'One does what one has to, when needs be,' and it was need that made it necessary for my Mam to do laundry. With Dad gone and me still at school, Mam had to try and keep us going. We were lucky that Dad had always managed to put a bit away for a rainy day. I remember him saying that. 'Put this in the jar,' he'd say, giving me some coins, 'They're for the rainy day,' he'd explain, always with a smile as though he never really expected it to rain. So I'd take the coins and drop them one by one into the huge, dark-green demi-john, loving the clinky noise they made. And from time to time now, Mam would dip into the hoard, tipping the jar over and letting a few coins trickle out, taking only enough for essentials and returning the others, looking up at me as she dropped them back, saying sadly, 'For the rainy day, son.'

'Yes, Mam,' I'd say, and watch her as she fondled the money knowing Dad had handled it too.

BOOK TWO

8

'Roll up! Roll up! Roll up!' Fergal Slattery called, his smile wide and generous, his beady little eyes calculating and steely, unable to hide the avarice of a man who lived off the misfortune of others. He was dressed in black despite the heat of the day, and a wide-brimmed black hat was jammed on to his big, square face. He looked like an old-time preacher and knew it; he modulated his voice into a kind of sing-song, quavering it from time to time for effect.

'Come on now, ladies and gents. Move closer so we can get the show on the road,' he called, pulling the crowd towards him by gesturing with his arms. He stood on the dray in the centre of the yard, and by his side, squatting on an upturned wooden butter-box, Ron Murray had his pencil poised to take down bids. Two chickens perched on the shafts of the dray, unafraid, enjoying the sunshine. Leghorns they were, old and past laying, and too tough for eating: broilers the women called them.

'Are you waiting for me to melt or what?' Fergal Slattery wanted to know, a note of irritation creeping into his preacher's voice. The Loftus sale should be a good one, and he had been looking forward to it. He found it difficult to give time to his usual pre-sale banter which put everyone in good humour and made them spend more than they intended.

'Right then, Ron. What's the first lot we have to offer these good folks?'

And the crowd, even those who were not interested,

pressed forward, ogling old Mrs Ballerman's rocking chair which Christie Slattery, Fergal's eldest son, held aloft.

Watching from the doorway of the house, leaning against the jamb, Dan Loftus had a silly smile on his face. In the two years since Deirdre's death he had changed little. If anything he looked a little younger, as though madness had granted him the compensation of youthfulness, and this added to the fear the villagers now had of him.

The farm, of course, had deteriorated rapidly. The cattle, unmilked, had contracted mastitis and were long since gone. The fields and hedges were wild and overgrown. Fences and walls had collapsed. The house too showed the signs of neglect: windows were cracked, the paintwork peeled off and hung like loose skin from the walls, and the roof had taken to leaking again. Only the small flower garden he had created for Deirdre seemed orderly: the flowers, untended, had seeded themselves and kept the weeds suffocated. In summer there was a haphazard profusion of blooms, and the colour was all the prettier for that. Sometimes Dan would pick huge bunches of these flowers, jam them into any containers he could find and position them in the house, an arrangement in each room, incongruously.

It was Uncle Tom, old Mrs Ballerman's brother, the politician, who had arranged for the furniture and farm implements to be sold off. He had tried to get Dan committed to an institution and to dispose of the farm also, but had failed. The judge, a country man who hadn't set foot in the city since his student days, knew what a home and land meant to a man, even a mad man, and said no, but he granted permission for effects to be sold to pay off Dan's outstanding bills, and he warned Tom that he would be keeping an eye on Dan to make sure he wasn't harassed or duped.

46

And as he left the bench the judge winked at Dan, and Dan winked back, thinking it was the proper thing to do.

'And a right good bargain you've got there, Missus, and no mistake,' Fergal Slattery said to Mrs Dawson, who had just paid four shillings for a tea-set of cream porcelain with orange nasturtiums painted on the borders. 'What's next?' he asked, as Mrs Dawson simpered and looked gleeful as if she'd pulled the wool over the auctioneer's eyes.

Dan watched his possessions being sold with little interest. Maybe he didn't even realise they were his; and if he did, perhaps he thought it was just as well to be rid of them since he never used them and they cluttered up the place, complicating his life.

Rose and Mary Kelly, the twins, sauntered past him, and gave him a funny look, giggling to each other, their big young breasts bouncing with jollity. Mary leaned towards Rose's ear and whispered, 'Wow,' and Rose hooted with laughter. 'Those hands! Did you see them?' Mary whispered. 'I saw them,' said Rose, and they both laughed some more because in their teenage logic big hands meant a big cock and they were of a time when big cocks were both comic and fascinating.

Dan laughed too, but wasn't sure why. He often did that: laughed when he heard other people laugh. Still laughing, he swung on his heel and went into the cool of the near empty house. Flies buzzed about his head and he swatted at them with his hand. They came mostly from the pantry where the hams still hung, all of them now covered in a green-blue fungus and shrunken to half their original size. Dan walked across the kitchen and shut the pantry door, trapping many of the gorged insects within.

That was all he did, he thought, but when he went to the front door again everyone was leaving and the sun had moved around to the back of the house, and the old chickens, the yard to themselves again, took dust-baths

47

while the rooster stood on tip-toe and flapped his ragged wings and shat spurts of excrement like this was part of his ritual. Dan frowned, confused as to why the people were leaving, just as he had been confused as to why they had come. He watched for a while as they wound their way homewards down the lane, and cocked his head trying to catch what they were saying. All he heard was a hum of conversation and the rattle of wheels in the ruts of mud hardened to concrete by the baking sun. He stood listening until all sound had gone and the dust had settled. Then, scratching himself under the arm, he walked across the yard and shut the gate, and forgot anyone had been there that day. He felt tired and yawned hugely and stretched. Time meant nothing to him. If he was tired he slept; if he wasn't he stayed awake. Somehow he had escaped the formula of day and night. And he was tired now and made his way slowly into the house again, and upstairs, wandering from room to room.

They had taken his bed and sold it, blankets and all, although they had dumped his filthy sheets in one corner and thrown the hard pillow on top of them. The bed old Mrs Ballerman had died in, the one Deirdre had taken to after Sergei's death, was still there, but Dan didn't fancy it. He liked the quilt on it though – pretty blues and yellows and pinks and greens – so he grabbed that and trundled downstairs. He spread the quilt in front of the range and lay down on it, curling himself up in front of the hearth like a great hound, and in his mind he heard the wood crackle in the unlit range.

9

'Where you goin', Dan?' Ferret Cassidy wanted to know.

'Goin' to Mrs Doyle for bread.'

'At this time of the night? She won't like that.'

'She said to come any time.'

'Not at night, you fool.'

'Any time is what she said.'

'That's just a way of talking.'

'That's what she said,' Dan insisted. 'Any time at all, she said.'

'It's after eleven. She'll be snoring her head off and won't take kindly to being roused,' Ferret warned.

Dan shrugged. 'Any time is what she said,' he pointed out, and trundled off, content that what he said was true.

'You're out and about late, Dan,' Mrs Doyle told him, her hair in paper curlers and fragments of sleep clinging to her eyelashes.

'You said any time.'

'I did. I did.'

Mrs Doyle was a kindly woman with pretensions to saintliness. Charity, she told herself, not cleanliness, was next to godliness, but she was selective and changed her mind on a whim. She had as keen a tongue as the next woman, and gave far better than she got, but she liked Dan and had looked after him, giving him bread she baked and sometimes making him a pie with the offcuts of the meat she bought for herself. 'And,' she said now, 'I've got you what I promised.'

Dan frowned.

'Don't you remember?'

Dan shook his head and grinned.

'The bicycle! Don't you remember I promised I'd keep my eye out for an old bike for you to get around on?'

Dan didn't remember, but he beamed anyway.

'Well, I got you one. It's a lady's bike, I'm afraid, but I dare say you won't be minding that.' She handed him half a loaf of soda bread wrapped in newspaper. 'It's in the shed there. You just take it and away you go now.'

Dan almost collided with the Kelly twins as he wobbled his way out of the village, taking the road towards town, away from his home, practising.

'Jesus God! You're like the devil himself riding out of the gloom,' Rose told him.

'Eijit! Putting the hearts across us like that,' Mary said, looking as though she'd quite enjoyed the fright.

The twins had been to a dance in town and were all dolled up in their best clothes, their hair braided and a smearing of Max Factor on their faces. They were, as they put it, fed up and frustrated that all the trouble they'd gone to had been unrewarded. There just weren't enough men around. That was the trouble. Not enough men that a girl would want to be bothered with anyway. Besides, grand though they might look in the village, in the town the girls smirked at them, and talked about them out of the corners of their mouths, saying how silly they looked in all those frills and flounces. And that hair! Jesus, Granny did her hair that way a hundred years ago! And the long walk home didn't improve matters, making them hot and irritable and catty, and them knowing that their Dad, Jim Kelly, would be waiting for them, well drunk, and calling them a 'right pair of hussies flaunting their bits at anyone who sniffed around'.

Arms linked, their hips akimbo, tightening their

buttocks, the girls blocked Dan's way, and decided to have some fun. Mary reached out and started to stroke Dan's hand as it rested on the handlebars. 'When you goin' to make love to us, Dan?' she asked.

'Don't,' Rose hissed.

'Shush,' snapped Mary. 'When, Dan? When you goin' to screw us silly and hard?'

Dan blinked.

'I hear you're really good at it,' Mary went on.

'Mary,' Rose hissed again.

Mary's fingers were on Dan's knee now and started walking towards his crotch.

Dan looked puzzled, but he was smiling and quite enjoying himself.

'How big's your cock, Dan?' Mary asked.

'Pretty big,' Dan told her after some thought. 'No bigger though than any Leghorn rooster,' he added truthfully.

For a second there was silence and then the girls hooted with laughter, rocking back and forth on their very high heels.

'What you girls up to?' Ferret Cassidy, four rabbits on a pole over his shoulder, came upon them unnoticed, snipping their laughter to a gurgle.

The girls squirmed. Rose tried to haul Mary into retreat, but Mary was having none of that. Brazen, she was called. A right brazen hussy, her Dad called her. Stand there and lie to your face as brazen as you like she would, he'd say, and there'd be a little bit of envy in his voice.

'We're only talking to Dan,' Mary told Ferret.

'Huh,' Ferret grunted. 'I saw you,' he said.

'You saw nothin'. Nothin' at all, Ferret Cassidy. And don't you go making up stories about us or I'll set our Dad on you,' Mary said like her Dad was a guard-dog or something.

51

'You take off, Dan,' Ferret said, 'You don't want to be messing with these two.'

Dan thought about this for a while, and finally seemed to agree. He set off towards home, using the bike like a scooter, pushing himself along with one foot, ping-pinging the little bell when he felt like it.

'That Dan Loftus is going to find himself in hot water if he isn't careful,' Ferret Cassidy told his wife, waking her up to tell her, which she didn't think a lot of.

'Dan's all right,' Mrs Cassidy said, turning over and pulling the blankets down because of the heat.

'*He* might be all right but them others'll land him in trouble and that's for sure.'

'What others?'

'Them Kelly twins.'

'That pair!'

'That pair,' Ferret said, taking off his socks and hanging them out the window to get rid of the stink.

'What have they got to do with it?' Mrs Cassidy wanted to know, suddenly interested and propping herself up on an elbow.

'I caught them at it,' Ferret said, down to his under-clothes.

'At what?'

'Messing with him.'

'What d'you mean – messing with him?'

Ferret collapsed into the bed. 'You know.'

'What?'

'Messing.'

It was one of those curious, balmy nights which sometimes, perhaps by accident, find their way on to the Atlantic coast, rest for a while and then blow away to their proper climes. The sky had been a brilliant carmine earlier in the evening and even now the dark blue was tinged with red, and this redness reflected itself in the sea, making it seem warm. Bats swarmed from their hiding places and gorged themselves on the insomniac insects which still fluttered about, fooled by the warmth. The birds were restless too, some of them chirping drowsily as they waited for sleep to come, and somewhere, high, high in the heavens, a nightingale put the songs of his cousins to shame.

Dan sat on the wall of the bottom field and stared out to sea, sniffing the air like a pointer, his bicycle propped beside him. Out at sea someone called, and Dan waved although he could see nothing and did not know whether the caller was greeting him or just cursing some tangle in his nets. Not that it mattered. Dan was liable to wave at anyone, and in his mind he was waving, standing by the door of the cowshed waving, waving cheerfully to a child, a boy in short trousers and with plimsolls on his sockless feet and a white shirt frayed at the collar, a boy of about six who sat atop the gate out of the yard and wriggled his body to make it swing back and forth.

'I want you to stop seeing so much of Dan Loftus,' my Mam said, concerned. She'd just started reading *To Kill a Mockingbird* and visions of the unfortunate Boo loomed large and frightening in her mind, I suppose. She was a great reader, my Mam. She read anything she could get her hands on, and she really got involved in the books, making the characters alive, crying at their sorrows and laughing with them at their joys. There were lots of words she didn't understand, but she had a dictionary and she'd spend ages rooting out the definitions and repeating them to herself until they were firmly lodged in her mind.

'Why?'

'Because I say so,' Mam told me which was her way of saying she couldn't think of a good reason. 'Anyway, I'm sure he doesn't want to be bothered.'

'He likes me going to see him.'

Mam got suspicious. 'What makes you think that?'

'He said so.'

'What did he say?'

'Well, nothing. But it's *like* he said so.'

Mam looked relieved. 'What nonsense you to talk some-times,' she said, and went back to putting a patch on the seat of my everyday pants, clucking her tongue and adding, 'I've never known a boy get through the seat of his trousers like you do.' Then she looked over the top of her spectacles. 'It's just that Dan's not right. He can't be sure what he's doing, and I fear for you.'

'He's nice, Mam.'

'I'm not saying he's not nice, child,' Mam said, and I could see that, in her way, she was pleased with me for finding Dan nice. 'But he's – well, whimsical.'

'What's that?'

'Odd.'

'You mean mad.'

Mam winced. 'I mean different.'

'Can't I go and see him sometimes?'

'No.'

'Just sometimes?'

'No.'

'Aw, Mam – '

'No,' Mam snapped.

'Just once in a while?'

I thought I knew how to get around Mam. Ever since my Dad had died and left the two of us alone I had learned that by using a pleading, jokey voice like Dad had used when he wanted something, I could usually get what I wanted. 'Just sometimes?'

'Here's your pants,' Mam said. 'And the answer's still no.'

'Are you really mad, Dan?'

54

Dan looked at me and put his foot against the gate to stop me swinging on it.

'They're all saying you are, you know.'

Dan lifted me off the gate and swung me on to his shoulders.

'What's it like being mad, Dan?'

We were off around the farmyard at a gallop, me screaming and Dan hollering, lifting his long legs high at the knee like a trotting horse. Only when he was out of breath did he stop and lower me safely to the ground. Then, without looking at me again, he dashed off into the farmhouse, slamming the door behind him as if I'd made him angry. Maybe, I thought, he was mad.

Dan had meandered farther than usual, out of the valley and over the north hill, but he had done so on purpose and had plodded on doggedly, head bent, until he came to the stream. It was the best stream in the world for fishing. Down its soft-flowing length were pools crammed with trout, and sometimes salmon. So plentiful were the fish that you could catch them with anything, any sort of line with any sort of hook, even string with a bent pin. Sometimes Dan sat there all day, a string tied to his toe, dozing, becoming alert only when the string tugged and then he yanked the fish on to the bank and smashed its head between two flat stones, stones he kept there for that purpose, stones he hid when he went away, stones stained with the blood of hundreds of fish. When he thought of it he brought matches and would light a small fire with last year's bracken and twigs and cook the fish, but often he would eat it raw, sucking on the flesh as if it were citrus, and washing it down with handfuls of clear water from the stream. Before he left he would place the bones and heads in small piles, maybe six or seven, and at night secretive little animals would dine, and Dan liked the idea of that although he never bothered to wait and see them enjoy their free feast.

That day, though, he wasn't going to use string. He was going to tickle the trout. Tickling was something he didn't often do although he enjoyed it more than hooking. He kept it for special occasions, but what was so special about any time he did it only he knew. Probably, it had something to do with his mood: if his mood was right the occasion was special.

He lay on his belly and gazed into the water, keeping very still and waiting for the fish to settle after being disturbed by his shadow. Funny things fish, the thought struck him. Emotionless. Never looking happy or sad. Contrary too, surviving in water and dying in air. He slid a hand into the water and left it floating there, palm upwards. Soon there were fish coming curiously to examine this strange intruder, nosing the tips of his fingers with their snouts. Oddly, the youngsters were the least adventurous, hanging back, allowing their elders to take all the risks. Dan set his sights on a nice, plump two-pounder, waiting for it to manoeuvre itself over his hand. He would have waited all day to catch that one now he'd settled on it, but he didn't have to. Within minutes he was stroking the trout's belly, putting it into a trance, then suddenly grasping it and flicking it from the water in one lightning deft action. He didn't apologise as he smashed the stone down on the trout's head, but he said, 'Thank you, fish', which was just as good, better really since it meant more to him.

'When you goin' to take me fishing with you, Dan?' I had asked earlier that summer.

Dan had cackled and shaken his head.

'What's to laugh at?'

'You're too young by an inch,' Dan said, whatever that meant.

'That's daft,' I said, feeling superior even at that age, superior to Dan anyway.

Dan leaned against the gate to stop me swinging it, and stared really hard at me like he was looking *through* me and out the other side. Then he closed his eyes for a minute and when he opened them there was a look in them I'd never seen before: a really *wise* look, although I don't

57

think I'd have called it that then. I remember thinking it was like as if someone else had come into his body, someone who knew everything, and ousted the mad Dan for a while or shifted him to one side anyway.

'Fish is curious things,' Dan told me. 'They's holy things, you know. There's folks who believe they's got spirits like humans. Down the coast road there's a village that counts on the fish for their living. And when the boats come in the eldest child of the youngest fisherman in the first boat home will take the bones of the largest fish back to the shore and offer them back to the sea, and say, "Go safely and become whole, fish. And return next year so that our bellies may be filled with your flesh and our hearts filled with your spirit." They *own* the waters, you see, fish do. The sea and the rivers and streams and all.'

That was the way Dan talked when his madness was shunted out of him for a bit.

Anyway, when he'd eaten the fat trout, and had a drink from the stream, Dan lay back for a rest, his hands folded behind his head. He didn't mean to fall asleep but he did, and it was close on dusk when he awoke. 'Blast me for a fool,' he told himself and started to get himself ready for the trek home, urinating and brushing the grass from his clothes tidily. He'd just finished piling the bones when he heard the voices. He shook his head. He often heard voices. Much of the time they were chatterings within his head, and it took him a while to decide these voices were real. These were real and no mistake: little grunts and squeals and loudly whispered words. Dan moved on all fours through the rushes like a predator, stopping from time to time to cock his head and listen. The sounds got louder. He sat back on his haunches and spread the rushes with his hands, poking his head into the clearing.

'Fucking God,' Eamonn Boyle swore, leaping off Mary

58

Kelly, his hard little penis wilting to a flabby miserable thing.

'Oh, shit,' said Des Keogh, rolling over on his back off Rose Kelly, covering his eyes with one hand and his penis with the other.

'What you doin' sneaking up and spying on us, you crazy bastard?' Eamonn demanded, furious at being interrupted. It had taken some cajoling to get the Kelly twins to drop their knickers: despite their foul talk and glib way they were pretty prudish when it actually came to doing anything, going the whole way anyway. 'I'm goin' to kick your fucking head in,' Eamonn added, buttoning his fly. 'Give us a hand, Des, for Christ's sake.'

Both young men were on Dan before he knew what was happening, kicking him cruelly and clouting him with their fists. He rolled himself into a ball like a hedgehog, tasting blood in his mouth as it trickled there from his nose. Eamonn's boots had metal tips and Dan could hear them cracking on his bones.

'Leave him, Des,' Rose Kelly called. 'You'll kill him before you know it.'

'Shush,' said Mary, her eyes glistening at the sight of Dan's pain.

'I won't shush,' Rose snapped and stood up, pulling at Des Keogh's arm, urging him to stop. 'Kicking him is one thing, killing him's another.'

Perhaps it was the word 'killing' that gave Dan the idea. He uncurled himself and flopped over on his back with a mighty groan, spreading his arms wide. He kept his eyes closed, and held his breath, and gave a few artistic twitches for good measure.

'Jesus!' Rose exclaimed, holding her flushed face in her hands. 'You *have* killed him.'

'No we haven't.'

'Yes you have. Oh, Jesus, look – he's stopped breathing.'

'He's moving, for Christ's sake.'

59

'Them's just those death jumps.'

'Shit, Eamonn,' Des Keogh put in, 'I think she's right.'

'Let's get out of here then.'

'And just leave him?'

'Sure, just leave him. Nobody'll miss him.'

'Somebody'll surely find him. Then what?'

'Not for ages they won't.'

'But when they do?'

'Shit, they won't know it was us, will they? Not if we all keep our gobs shut.'

'Let's get going then.'

Dan heard them scamper away, and managed a wily little cackle to himself. He sat up and wiped the blood from his nose with his sleeve. His ribs were painful, as was his groin, but it was quite an interesting pain he decided, and it seemed important to him that he remember this brutality although he wasn't sure why. Anyway, he felt himself all over and memorised the places that hurt, making a list of them in his mind and ticking them off like a shopping list.

He stayed by the river that night, not sleeping, just lying on his back, pretending to pluck stars from the heavens, holding them for a minute before releasing them, sending them skyward again by blowing on his fingers.

It must have been close to four in the morning when he decided he'd had enough of his celestial game, and that it was time to go home. Without thinking he took the long road round, the road that led through the village. Yet when he got as far as the cemetery he decided to scout around the houses, avoiding the main street. The backs of houses always told you more about the people who lived in them than the front, he thought. People always had the fronts of their houses looking pretty for others to see and admire and, even, be jealous of. But the backs (often unpainted and neglected) really gave them away, didn't they? Yes, he told himself, and stopped and peered at the house he was passing. By coincidence it was the Kelly house, and in the corner room the light of a night-candle glowed. It was the twins' room: the two girls slept together in a big double bed but even this proximity to each other didn't allay the strange fear they had of the dark, and every night they kept the candle burning until dawn. 'Burn the bloody house down those two halfwits will,' their Dad muttered. 'What's to be afraid of with the dark?' But the girls couldn't tell him. 'Well, if you two wake up and find yourselves burnt to death, don't come complaining to me,' their Dad told them. 'We won't,' the girls chorused, finding nothing odd about his statement.

The light attracted Dan, just as light attracts timid creatures and insects. Stealthily he made his way to the window and peered in. In the candlelight it looked warm and cosy and Dan liked it so he smiled. Unluckily Rose woke from her sleep at that moment; she'd had bladder trouble for some time. She swung her feet out of bed, and then saw Dan's face leering at her from outside. For a minute she froze, sitting there, her legs dangling, her mouth open. Then she screamed.

Mary sat bolt upright in the bed. 'God Almighty, Rose, what's the matter with you?'

'I seen him,' Rose wheezed, looking white as a sheet, her eyes bulging, gaping at the window from which Dan had vanished, having taken off like a whippoorwill at the sound of Rose's piercing scream.

'Seen who?'

'Him. The ghost of him leering at me from the window there.'

Mary stared at the window. 'There's nothing there, you fool.'

'Not now. But he was. Dan Loftus was watching us, just waiting for a chance to come in and get us and have his revenge.'

'Would you not be so daft, Rose – '

'I'm telling you, Mary, his ghost was there as large as life. You could be dead now if I hadn't seen him and frightened him off.'

The girls' Dad thumped on the wall and roared at them to be quiet after asking what the hell was going on in there.

'Will you get back into bed for the love of God, Rose.'

Rose got back into bed forgetting about her bladder. 'You don't believe me, do you?'

'If you saw him it means the boys didn't kill him.'

'It was his ghost. It looked like nothing human, Mary.'

And the funny thing was that although they saw Dan regularly after that the girls were never quite convinced he was real, always looking at him askance in case they could spot some evidence of ghostliness. And their boyfriends, too, were wary, giving Dan a wide berth in case he really was a spirit and possessed of dreadful magical powers. People noticed how the four of them shifted uneasily when Dan came along, and they heard little snippets of what was said about him, and all this added to Dan's reputation for weirdness and lumbered him with an imagined potency of which he knew nothing. Parents used him as a means of terrifying recalcitrant children into submission: 'You do what you're told, or we'll have the ghost of Dan Loftus come and deal with you.'

But most of the children only pretended to be afeared, making faces of terror by widening their eyes and pleading in pathetic voices not to have a terrible visitation by Dan Loftus foisted upon them. But they weren't in the least scared: far from it. They determined to turn the tables on their parents, to get Dan Loftus on their side in case he might help them in the future with his strange, imagined powers. And to this end they were especially nice to him, leaving gifts of food and home-made beer and wine for him at the gate, with notes saying who had left them, so that Dan would know the names when the time came for him to repay their generosity.

'*Now* they're saying you're a ghost,' I told Dan.

Dan put his arms in the air and waved them, pulling a terrible face. 'Ghost,' he said, by way of explanation I think.

'Don't seem like a ghost to me,' I told him.

Dan grinned.

'Not mad either.'

Dan's grin widened.

'You know something, Dan? You're the only friend I've got. Honest.'

I don't know if Dan understood that, or if he was just in one of his better moods, but there and then he hugged me and kissed the top of my head.

I I

Only when the evenings got chilly did the circus up tents and leave the city. PETER CAVANAGH'S TRAVELLING CIRCUS was emblazoned on the sides of most of the wagons. Only those with bars on their sides, like mobile cages, didn't advertise, the pacing, snarling leopards and tigers and scrawny lions being alluring enough to draw the crowd. But not in the city when the evenings got chilly. Townsfolk liked their comfort; they liked to be warm and cosy even when faced with the possibility of the Great Armondo hurtling to his death from the trapeze, or Saluddin, Prince of Tyre no less, being irretrievably launched into the stratosphere from a cannon.

So when the weather changed and autumn gave its first hint of winter, the circus travelled through the countryside visiting every minor village and town on its way to winter quarters. And the first frost had burnished the sloes, and made the Brussels sprouts tighten their leaves when the caravan trundled into the village and set up camp on the playing field, opposite the church.

In no time at all the Big Top had been erected and the stalls unfolded, and the Fattest Woman in the World was in business, as was Madame Calill, the midget fortune teller who was a card-carrying member of the Little Folk of America, and the marvellous Lucifer who ate fire and razor-blades and crunched glass, spitting the shards into a bowl before swallowing a sword to a dramatic drum roll. And there was a small tent, the same colour as the

Big Top but much, much smaller, which had a banner saying EXOTIC CREATURES waving from its top. It housed a llama which spat with deadly accuracy, and a black bear with a white vee like a mayor's chain on its chest which sat on its buttocks and sratched, and a pair of green monkeys with pink backsides which eternally de-flead each other and ate the offending insects all in separate cages, of course, and all looking as though they wished the gawkers would be on their way and let them get a decent, unwitnessed sleep.

Without exception, everyone in the village went to the one and only performance, just as everyone without exception went to Midnight Mass on Christmas Eve, and the dance on the night of Harvest Thanksgiving. Well, almost everyone. Mrs Dillon didn't go but she went nowhere. She was a hundred and two as near as anyone could guess, and deaf and blind, and didn't know for sure herself if she was dead or alive. And Mike Gerraty didn't go, but he didn't count because he went nowhere that cost him money, being so mean that he'd had his coffin made and paid for twenty years ago in case the price of timber went up. But everyone else went, even the babies, carried by their mothers and suckled during the performance.

Mind you, it wasn't quite the same show that the folk in the cities saw. It lasted only an hour instead of two, but the prices were slashed in half and everyone agreed they got their money's worth and went home well satisfied, marvelling at the exploits of the tight-rope walkers, chuckling at the antics of the clown, and the younger boys trying to cartwheel and somersault and sometimes succeeding in doing both and vowing that *they* would join the circus when they grew up.

Dan was beside himself with glee when he saw the circus wind over the hill and down the steep road to the village. It wasn't as if he looked forward to its coming from year to year. Indeed, as soon as the circus upped stakes and left it was instantly obliterated from his mind. So, each year it was like a grand, new, unforeseen delight, and each year he marvelled anew at the jugglers and tumblers and high-fliers, unaware that he had been mesmerised by these same acts the year before.

'Let's hear your clapping then for the beautiful Grace sisters,' the ring-master demanded as the three sisters finished their contortions and skipped out of the ring through hoops a-glitter with tinsel, as were their skimpy costumes. The audience clapped and some of the bright young sparks whistled, more in derision than praise for the Grace sisters were getting on a bit now, and their once-shapely legs were fattening up, their thighs rubbed together and their bottoms had dropped.

'Now then,' the ringmaster said into his megaphone, holding up a hand to stop the applause which had already withered away but perhaps still rang in his ears from some earlier, grander era. 'Now then, the act I know you've all been waiting for. The chance for you young fellas to show what you're made of.'

A great ooooooh went up and an unexpected nervous tension seemed to descend on the crowd. The girls nudged each other and giggled, and pulled faces at their boy-friends who sat close to the ringside, while they, the girls, wedged between mothers, sat higher up at what was deemed a respectable distance.

'Yes, ladies and gentlemen. It's Gustav and the unbeatable Harold!' the ringmaster roared, and into the ring strode Gustav and the unbeatable Harold.

Everyone cheered like crazy. Gustav bowed deeply from the waist. And the unbeatable Harold, an ape of monstrous proportions, thumped his chest and rocked from foot to foot on the end of his rattling chain, his eyes gleaming.

'Right, now,' the ringmaster said, 'And who's going to

66

be first? Don't forget it's a crisp ten-pound note for anyone who can hold Harold down for ten seconds. A pound a second, you might say. Surely some of you brawny young lads can do that?' Maybe some of those brawny young lads could but they weren't all that anxious to try, it seemed. They elbowed their companions and said, 'You go,' and 'No, you go.' Then someone said, 'Get Dan to go,' and all of a sudden a chant went up: 'We want Dan! We want Dan!' Soon the big top was ringing with the cry and Dan, bemused at such attention, was on his feet before he knew it, and stepping into the ring, and beaming as everyone cheered. He pulled off his tattered pullover and his shirt and his dirty vest and threw them on to the ground, and everyone cheered louder. 'Get him, Dan,' someone called, and everyone took that up, 'Get him, Dan. Get him, Dan.'

Dan took up an odd crouched position and waited. Gustav had a word in Harold's ear and unhooked the chain. Harold crouched too. The crowd sucked in its breath and waited.

Dan and Harold circled each other, still crouched, in a grotesque schottische. Both of them grunted a lot, each seeming to imitate the other. Then, without warning, Harold lunged and grabbed Dan, pinning his arms to his sides, and the pair of them set off in a wild polka about the ring while the young bucks rose from their seats and stomped their feet and roared their approval and guffawed, and the ringmaster, sweating, beamed at the extraordinary success of his exhibition.

For Dan, however, it was another kettle of fish. The ape's embrace was phenomenal, forcing the breath from his lungs, and he could feel his heart pumping wildly and his ribs set to crack at any moment. The stench from Harold's matted fur made him want to vomit. The more the audience roared and laughed the more frightened Dan became; the more they applauded and encouraged him

67

the closer he came to panic. Finally, without thinking, some strange instinct guiding him, he sank his teeth into the ape's neck and worried at it like a demented terrier. He tasted the animal's blood oozing into his mouth. He felt it relax its grip. Dan wanted to let go but his jaws simply would not open. Harold collapsed, pulling Dan on top of him, and thrashed about in the sawdust of the arena, and still Dan clung on, his face and torso now covered in blood. He felt no pain as Gustav ran towards them wielding Harold's chain and bringing it down with all his force on Dan's back. Quite the opposite. Dan found himself liking it: it goaded him on, and he was ripping mouthfuls of flesh from the luckless beast, spitting them out, then savaging again.

Some of the women screamed and turned away, but the men seemed quite transfixed, their eyes glazed as they witnessed Dan kill Harold. Something about the sheer horror of it all appealed to them and made them randy. Most of them were still standing, mesmerised, when Gustav finally dragged Dan off by forcing the chain around his neck and heaving backwards.

For some time Dan stood there panting, then he spun on his heel and trotted from the tent, people moving quickly out of his way.

The circus didn't wait for dawn to move on. They packed and left silently in the night. Yet because they were circus people and honest they left a ten-pound note on the spot where Harold had been killed, paying the price despite their grief.

'Now you know why I won't have you going to visit that Dan Loftus,' my Mam said.

'He wouldn't kill me,' I insisted.

'Huh. That's probably what that monkey said to its mother,' Mam said with a wicked twinkle in her eye.

'Aw, Mam.'

'You can aw Mam me as much as you like, young man, but you let me catch you within a mile of Dan Loftus and I'll give you a hiding the likes of which you've never had.'

Of course, in the retelling, what Dan had done that night was greatly exaggerated so that in the end he was said to have torn the animal limb from limb. 'You should have seen it,' the talk went to strangers. 'Broke him up like was twigs for kindling, and taking big swigs of his blood to keep him going.'

Or: 'Like something possessed, he was. And I'll tell you what's more: his body swelled up and his teeth grew into fangs while he was demolishing the ape, and that's no word of a lie.'

All of which gave Dan a certain kudos. Nobody harassed him any more, and nobody taunted him to his face. Even Mr Biddlecombe, the grocer, no longer told him to get his stupid arse out of the shop and come back when he had money. Oh no, 'It's sugar you want, is it, Dan? Well, here you are. You just pay me the next time you're in. Haven't you been a customer of mine for long enough for me to trust you?' Although the leering smile did falter when Dan said he'd like some tea, too, to go with the sugar. And perhaps a packet of those sweety biscuits, the ones with the custardy cream in the middle?

Polly Gibbons saw Dan going home with his sugar and tea and biscuits, juggling them, and hop-skip-jumping up the lane. So she said she'd seen Dan Loftus having a fit, and by the time it got back to Mrs Biddlecombe, the grocer's wife (who just sat in the shop and gossiped and crocheted), Dan had been foaming at the mouth and carrying on like he had rabies.

That was the way it was from then on: everything blown out of proportion. There were those who envied Dan despite his affliction since he was what they called 'a

69

somebody', and they knew that never in their lives would they be a somebody. And they'd die, and within weeks nobody would hardly remember their name. But Dan was the stuff of crazy folklore, and many begrudged him this, irked that their good clean way of life would be forgotten while his lunatic carry-on would be recalled and embellished and related by firesides for generations to come.

In any case, it was inevitable that it was that way, always exaggerating everything Dan did, I mean. If they related things without embellishment as they actually happened they wouldn't have had an excuse to kill him, would they? And they surely had to kill him: it was the only way, you see, that they could grab a bit of his legend and prove, as every man needs to, that they did, in fact, once exist.

12

People have a thousand obscure ways of signifying the changes of season, and the villagers were no different. They used the birds and trees, the sky and the sea, usually pretty gloomily, death and the cold being blamed on the innocent activities of the cuckoo, the fertility of the rowan, the colours of the dusk, the whimsical interpretations of the sighs of the sea. But there was one infallible indication of the coming of the first frost which was unique to the village. In the autumn, regardless of what the weather was like, when the first smoke curled from Olly Carver's chimney you could stake your life that the next morning there would be a fine white covering of frost on the ground. It never failed. How Olly knew was anyone's guess, but know he did, and once smoke was spotted from his chimney all the other fires and ranges in the village would be rekindled, and the old people cursed poor Olly gently, blaming him for the coming of winter, but they did so quietly, to themselves, keeping their curses intimate.

Olly Carver lived some way outside the village, almost as far as Dan Loftus but in the other direction, away from the sea and high up in the hills. They said he had killed his wife trying for a son since she'd died in childbirth after bearing him thirteen daughters. Nobody said as much to his face, for he was a surly man of quick, unpredictable temper; he had a shotgun and two rifles and was the keenest shot anyone had ever seen, yet his prowess with a gun was a well-kept secret, coming to light only some three years after his wife had died. It was a Friday evening

71

and Olly had come to the shop with Heather, his eldest daughter, to collect the shopping: she carried the basket, Olly his gun in case he saw a rabbit ripe for the pot. On Friday evenings the men gathered in Biddlecombe's shop to chatter about the goings-on of the week. There were about a dozen of them there when Olly and Heather walked in. They stopped talking. They eyed Olly, they eyed Heather too, but in a different way for she was a strapping girl, buxom and bosomy, with a look about her that sent shivers of excitement up and down their spines.

'Been shooting?' Mr Biddlecombe asked for want of something to say.

'No,' Olly said, waiting while Heather loaded up the basket.

'Not that you'd shoot much with that,' said Mr Biddlecombe, trying to be witty, jerking his baldy head towards the old Enfield with its cracked stock.

Olly gave him a baleful look and took to stroking the gun like he expected it to react favourably to his caress. 'You think not,' he asked finally. 'And you wouldn't be putting a few shillings where your mouth is, I suppose?'

'Meaning?'

'How much d'I owe you for those?' Olly asked pointing to the groceries.

Mr Biddlecombe consulted his list. 'Three pounds, five shillings and eightpence. Exactly.'

'Well, then. You name a target and if I hit it first time I get the goods free.'

'You're on,' said Mr Biddlecombe.

'And I get the same amount free next week.'

Mr Biddlecombe looked doubtful. The thought of losing money fair near broke his heart. He looked, too, as though he suspected some plot was being hatched against him, and somehow everyone in his shop was in league, ready to make a fool of him.

'That's only fair,' Pete Murphy said, taking his pipe

from his mouth and spitting on to the sawdusted floor. 'After all, he's lettin' you pick the target, isn't he?'

Mr Biddlecombe nodded.

'Well then, what you hedgin' for?'

Mr Biddlecombe made up his mind. 'You're on,' he said firmly, and stuck his hand out to be shaken.

Olly shook his hand. 'Pick your target,' he said.

Mr Biddlecombe looked around him. 'In here, you mean?' He sounded alarmed.

Olly shrugged. 'Why not? I won't hit nothin' else.'

'Hey look!' It was Pete Murphy again. 'Look. There,' he said, pointing with the stem of his pipe. 'There's a spider. Get him to shoot that from where he's standing.'

Mr Biddlecombe clearly liked the idea. He beamed. 'Right, then, Olly,' he said smugly. 'Shoot the spider.'

'You want me to kill it or take a leg off of it?' asked Olly, cocking his rifle and peering down the sights.

'Oh, very smart. Just hit it.'

'Meant what I said.'

'All right then. Just take a leg off of it. If you kill it I win – right?'

'Right,' said Olly and fired.

There was an unholy bang and the shop filled with smoke. The bottles and jars and tins jumped on the shelves and, for some reason, the cork flew out of the vinegar barrel.

'Jesus Holy Christ!' exclaimed Mr Biddlecombe, waving the smoke away from his face and hastening to replug the barrel. 'What you go and do that for anyway?' he demanded.

Olly just grinned. 'Go get your spider,' he said.

Me Biddlecombe looked stunned, as though he'd forgotten all about the wager. 'Oh. The spider. Yes,' he said finally and made to examine the spot where the spider had been, climbing clumsily on to a chair and peering at the wall, probing with a finger. Slowly he withdrew his

73

finger and turned slowly, looking very pleased with himself. 'I win,' he announced. 'Look for yourself. You've done killed the spider.' Olly shook his head without looking up. 'No I ain't.'

'Yes you bloody have.' Mr Biddlecombe turned back to the wall and pointed again. 'There's a hole from the bullet and there – come and look if you don't believe me – there's the mess that was the spider.' Olly continued to shake his head. 'That's just its shit,' he said. 'Little bugger shat himself just like you'd shit if I put a bullet that close to you.'

Mr Biddlecombe wondered if this was the conspiracy he had sensed earlier. He climbed off the chair and faced Olly, looking belligerent. 'A likely story.'

'You callin' me a liar?' Olly wanted to know calmly enough but slipping a finger in and out of the trigger guard ominously.

Mr Biddlecombe thought better of attack. 'No. But – '

'You'll find the spider on the shelf 'neath the hole.'

And sure enough that's where Mr Biddlecombe found the spider, on the shelf, between two jars of Vick, and one of its legs missing, blown clean off at the joint. And that was how Olly Carver got his reputation as a shot, and why people didn't argue with him despite the terrible way he treated his unfortunate daughters.

'Dan,' Olly said, and nodded by way of welcome.

'Olly,' Dan said, and nodded too, returning the greeting.

'You stoppin' or just passin'?'

'Stopping.'

'Better come inside then.'

Dan followed Olly into the house, sidestepping the children and the chickens.

'Get them young ones up to their beds,' Olly told Heather, or it might have been Myrtle or Hazel or Holly.

Dan smiled at the children as they filed obediently out of the room.

'And bring in the flagon,' Olly ordered. 'Sit yourself, Dan,' he added, poking at the fire to get it going.

Dan sat down. It was always the same procedure when he came to call, and he came to call quite often. Something told him Olly liked his company; and why wouldn't he, him with nothing but women to talk to? Always the younger children were sent to bed and the flagon of poteen brought in. They'd drink for a while and then Olly would start talking, and if Dan said anything Olly would listen like as if Dan was a wise old bird.

Heather or Myrtle or Hazel or Holly brought in the flagon and two glasses, handing one to Dan. Then she sat on the floor by her father's chair, curling herself up inconspicuously.

For a while, an hour maybe, the men drank, and then Olly set about talking. 'Thirteen of them and not a boy among the lot. Would you credit that?'

Politely Dan shook his head to say that he wouldn't credit that at all.

'I don't know what the good Lord had in mind for me, landing me with thirteen girls, and then taking the woman and leaving me to shepherd them.' Olly sucked heavily on his pipe, holding a matchbox over the bowl. 'It's a job, I can tell you,' he told Dan between puffs. 'Watching them all the while. Girls is tricky, you know. Still, virgins they were born and virgins they'll die,' Olly announced in a tone that suggested if he wasn't getting any his daughters weren't about to either.

Dan ogled the daughter curled at Olly's feet, and the look she returned was anything but virginal. Which was hardly surprising. Olly's four oldest daughters had a reputation second to none. God, they'd eat you alive given half a chance, and their father daft enough to think they'd never been touched! Lie down with anything they would.

And did. Indeed, when it came time for the young men to try their hand at it for the first time, you could count on Heather or Myrtle or Hazel or Holly to oblige and do a thorough job. But the girls were crafty enough to avoid pregnancy – so far, anyway. It was a rough sort of contraception, but it worked, and they had it down to a fine art. They would let the boy runt and thump away on top of them, then, with a quick twist of their bodies, hurl him off just as he spewed, and stand over him, laughing as he groaned in delight, and laughing louder as he came all over himself. Of course, there were stories that one of the girls, Heather most likely, had conceived, and had had a baby going off into the fields and dropping it, but it was only a story.

'Girls need loving,' Dan heard himself say, still eyeing the girl, and lusting after her, feeling the stirring in his loins and crossing his legs.

'They'll get their lovin' from the Lord,' Olly said, and his voice took on the tone of a Holy Joe.

Dan got argumentative. He shook his head. 'Not enough,' he said.

Olly scowled for a moment. Not, it appeared, in anger. It was his way of putting on a thinking face, and he was thinking seriously about what Dan had said. Whatever others might say would run off him without regard, but for some reason he took what Dan said as potentially carrying weight, as though Dan in his madness had an insight withheld from other mortals, wisdom and lunacy being akin his way of reckoning. 'You think not?' he asked finally.

'Sure,' Dan told him, sounding convinced but far from it now that he had been put on the spot.

Mind you, what Dan had in mind was a somewhat different sort of loving to what Olly might have imagined. From the moment his illness had struck, sex had played a big part in Dan's life. Not that he thought about it much.

76

He didn't. It just took over some part of his brain usually occupied with other things, and it seemed to follow the seasons, surging in the spring and summer, slackening off in the autumn and lying dormant in the cold winter months. Dan found nothing inhibiting or shameful about this. As with the animals, like the deer and the foxes and the badgers, it was a natural response to some urge within him, and if he could find no one to do it with he did it by himself.

But while many would have thought it unlikely, Dan did quite nicely, thank you. Indeed, he did better than most men in the village, his 'weirdiness' as it was called making him something of a catch: as Dolly Quinn said, like having it off with a murderer or a priest.

Olly emptied the remains of the alcohol into his glass and handed the bottle to the girl. 'Get another, Myrtle,' he said, and then, when Myrtle had gone from the room, he leaned forward and tapped Dan on the knee. 'It's the ideas they get that confound me,' he said, and winked and nodded as though the statement was profound. He was still nodding when Myrtle appeared in the doorway empty-handed and looking sulky. 'Can't find another,' she said.

'Dammit,' Olly said, and heaved himself out of his chair. 'Got through that batch at a clip,' he told Dan. 'Still,' he went on, smiling, 'there's plenty more under lock and key.'

With Olly gone, Myrtle advanced into the room, her eyes fixed on Dan in a sultry, questioning way. She stopped beside him and ran her fingers through his hair, and tickled the back of his ear. 'You're lovely, Dan,' she whispered.

Dan squirmed, and leaned away.

'Don't you want me, Dan?'

Dan did, but he wasn't about to say so, not with Olly in the house, and him the best shot with a gun in the whole wide world.

'I'll be waiting by the shed when you leave, Dan,' Myrtle told him and then, like a shot, crossed the room and squatted by her father's chair as Olly's footsteps echoed on the hall floorboards.

'There we go,' Olly said, beaming, holding a bottle aloft. 'Time you was in bed, girl,' he added, a look of suspicion creeping into his smile, making it waver and become almost sinister.

'Dan. Dan. Over here,' Myrtle called, waiting by the shed, true to her word. 'Come on. Quick!'

Dan loped across the yard, and Myrtle was on him in a flash, mauling him all over, and making little grunting noises and giving huge big sighs. Then she was sinking to the ground, pulling Dan down on top of her and writhing underneath him, and going 'Oooooh' as he penetrated her, and saying over and over, 'Oh Dan, oh Dan, oh Dan!'

And Dan was enjoying himself too, runting away like a man possessed, and making a noise about it into the bargain. Indeed, so noisy and busy were the pair of them that neither heard Olly come out of the house and across the yard. They had no idea he was there until he brought the flat side of the shovel down on Dan's buttocks with a fearsome wallop.

Dan never visited Olly again. Well, he tried, thinking to himself that what was done was done and was now over. But Olly ran him off, calling him a filthy dirty fucking shit, and waving his shotgun like he intended to use it. Myrtle didn't even look at him the next time their paths crossed in the village, although she had only the one eye to use, the other, swollen and black-blue being useless for the time being, and her being busy trying to keep the scarf over her head so people wouldn't notice how her hair had all been shaved off.

'Old Olly's caught poor Myrtle at it again,' the wags said sagely.

'Once for the hundred times she's got away with it.'

'Keepin' them for himself, most likely.'

'Lucky bugger.'

'Wonder who it was had her?'

'You can bet Olly doesn't know or there'd be a body lying somewhere.'

'Not decent, it isn't.'

'What?'

'Keepin' them girls up there and not sharing them.'

They thought that was really comical and guffawed a lot, opening their mouths and braying. And Dan, listening, laughed too because it seemed like a good idea to join in the happy merriment.

'Bet you'd like one, wouldn't you, Dan?' Freddy Carson asked, deciding that taunting Dan would be fun too, but instinctively rubbing his neck and keeping his hand there, not forgetting what Dan had done at the circus and knowing he was liable to take anyone for a monkey.

Dan stopped laughing and stared at Freddy, cocking his head to one side quizically.

'Wouldn't you, eh?'

'Wouldn't know what to do with one, he wouldn't, not if it was handed to him on a plate,' Mike Harvey said.

'God, I don't know,' Freddy didn't know. 'I've heard tell that the mad ones are divils for it, not having much else in their minds so to speak,' he concluded, taking a peep at Dan to make sure he hadn't taken offence.

Dan thought a lot about Myrtle in the weeks that followed. He forgot quickly about the pain of the shovel blade on his buttocks, but Myrtle's sighing and grunting lingered in his mind, and he used her image and her noises to help him when he enjoyed himself alone in his house. And that was a comfort, for the house, now that winter was coming, was cold and lonely, and the wind whistled through the broken windows and slammed doors and sent bits of paper and leaves scudding like hundreds of little ghostly footsteps wandering about, lost. And it was these lonely footsteps that often kept Dan awake, not the cold, so he played with himself to put them out of his mind, then curled himself up on the quilt in front of the unlit range and rocked himself, sometimes humming, to sleep.

And he curled himself up on the quilt in front of the unlit range and rocked himself to sleep, sometimes humming, in much the same way after he had decimated Mrs Biddy's chicken flock. Nobody blamed him for this, saying Tess Biddy must be the stupidest thing on two legs to let Dan loose with a hatchet in the first place, and wouldn't any of the lads in the village have done it for her had she had the sense to ask?

'How would you like a nice plump roast chicken, Dan? All stuffed with sage and onion?' Tess Biddy had asked Dan, thinking she'd give him one of the tough old birds which had stopped laying, while getting him to kill and pluck one of the tender young chickens for herself and that no-good husband of hers who couldn't do anything 'cept sit in his chair and nurse his gout and complain about what had become of him and he with an education as good as any a teacher in the country. Dan smiled widely and nodded.

'Well, you just kill that one for me and that one for yourself and pluck and clean them both and I'll roast the pair of them for us,' Tess Biddy told him, taking him into the yard and pointing out the two doomed birds. 'And don't you tear the skin while you're plucking them,' she warned. 'One thing I can't stand is torn skin on a chicken.'

It took Dan quite a while and quite a few handfuls of corn to catch the prey, putting one in a sack while he lured the other into his clutches. Then he honed the little hatchet nicely on the whetstone, feeling the edge with his thumb every so often until it was keened to his liking. He placed the chopping block squarely on the ground and laid the neck of the first chicken on it, keeping the bird still by holding its head in one hand and pressing its body against the block with his knee. Chop. The head was severed neatly. Dan let the chicken go, and off it went, headless, racing about the yard, scaring the life out of the other hens and cockerels. He did the same with the other chicken, and chuckled loudly as this, too, took off. It was a grand sight, he thought. Interesting how they managed so well without their heads, not bumping into anything but acting as if they could still see although their heads were on the ground beside him, motionless, with eyes staring fixedly at nothing.

Before he could stop himself Dan was chopping the heads off other chickens: the layers went, the pullets, the White Wyandotte rooster. Soon the yard was awash with decapitated fowls, charging about in eerie silence, their lovely white plumage speckled with scarlet blood.

'Haven't you fin – oh, my God!' Tess Biddy came out of her kitchen, her apron already on, wiping damp breadcrumbs from her fat little hands. 'Oh my God!' she screamed. 'Joe, would you get yourself out here and stop this madman before he ...' She couldn't think what he might do.

Dan looked up, smiled at her, and kept on chopping.

Joe came out and stood staring in a bewildered kind of way.

'Stop him,' Tess Biddy ordered.

'And have my own head chopped off?' Joe asked, not at all keen to do as he was bid, but nevertheless making a tentative move towards Dan. 'Hey, there, Dan,' he said.

Dan let another chicken go, and smiled at Joe. The two of them watched the bird flutter wildly towards the duck pond, somehow avoiding the carcasses that littered the yard. 'That's a fine job you've done, Dan,' Joe said, reaching out for the hatchet.

Dan smiled with pleasure.

'A really fine job,' Joe said.

Dan handed him the hatchet.

'You fucking great moron,' Joe roared now that he had the hatchet in his hand, raising it high over his head and aiming a vicious blow at Dan. Dan still smiling, stepped to one side, and the little axe swept by him and embedded itself in the soft flesh of Joe's thigh. 'Oh shit. Oh Christ. Oh Jesus,' Joe roared as the blood gushed from his wound. He dropped the hatchet and hobbled back towards his wife. 'See what you've made me do, you stupid woman?' he bellowed. 'Crippled myself, that's what I've done.'

'Crippled *you*? What about my chickens?' Tess Biddy demanded.

That was the story anyway, and the youngsters in the village had a great time for a few weeks going up to Mrs Biddy's house and saying their Mams had sent them to ask if, by chance, she'd have a few eggs for sale.

13

Father Tierney had succumbed to saintliness. He'd been having twinges in his chest for several months and Doctor McCann told him his heart was about to pack up. Of course the doctor didn't put it like that, but Father Tierney did, and he repeated it so often that he finally came to believe it, using it at the start of his sermon on Sundays to get everyone's attention. And it worked. The congregation never took their eyes off him in case he keeled over there and then in the pulpit, and who'd want to miss seeing a thing like that? 'My dear brethren,' he'd say softly, 'as you all know the good Lord has seen fit to weaken my heart and may call me to His side at any moment.' And then he'd pause, and wait for the sad ripple of remorse that inevitably skittered through the church. Only then would he get down to the meat of things.

Anyway, he got the idea that he wanted each male member of his flock, as he put it, to serve a Mass for him before he passed over. 'So that there's a real closeness between us,' he explained. 'A bond that I can carry with me to paradise.'

Well, saintly he might have become but he hadn't intended to include Dan in his cosy closeness. He hadn't thought of Dan as one of the flock although he came to Mass as regularly as anyone else, sitting at the back, gawping. But Dan heard about the priest's wish and thought it a very fine gesture indeed. So every Sunday he turned up at the sacristy door, waiting his turn, and showing no sign of resentment when Father Tierney said,

'Not *this* Sunday, Dan', and almost hoping his heart would give its final kick before the congregation ran out. But it didn't, and came the Sunday when Dan was the only one waiting by the sacristy door. Father Tierney stared at him in dismay, then sighed, and using the sigh as breath said, 'Yes, Dan. Today.'

Everything went swimmingly for a while. Kitted out in a crisp white surplice, Dan behaved himself admirably, kneeling when he should and standing when he should, and holding the edge of Father Tierney's alb as he mounted the steps so he wouldn't trip. He didn't make any of the responses though, but that didn't matter since Father Tierney was pretty relieved to do those himself. True, he knocked the little bell over and that caused some consternation since many of the congregation had been asleep and thought it was the Communion already. But apart from that there was no great error.

Until it was time for Dan to hand the wine and water to the priest for pouring into the chalice, that is. He shuffled to the side of the sanctuary and collected the cruets on their little glass tray and made it up the steps to the altar all right, even making certain that the tiny ladle-like spoon was there for the water. Certainly the cruets rattled a bit, but that had happened to everyone. He placed everything neatly on the edge of the altar, stood back, joined his hands reverently, and waited. He inclined his head properly when Father Tierney came to him with the chalice. He picked up the wine-cruet and handed it to the priest. He did the same with the water, putting them both back on the tray when the priest had finished. Father Tierney even managed a benign smile in Dan's direction. It could have been that which triggered off the mayhem that followed. Maybe Dan took it as an invitation, or maybe he thought he could share more fully in the sacrament, or maybe he was just thirsty. Whatever the reason, he eyed the wine left in the cruet and then, quite calmly, started to drink it. There was a massive hissing as the congregation sucked in its breath in unison. The noise was so vibrant that it stopped Father Tierney in his tracks. He turned and stared in puzzlement at his flock, then, following their eyes, he spun round and faced Dan who was draining the last drops of wine, his head thrown back, the cruet upended. Whether it was the shock of seeing this or just clumsiness that made Father Tierney drop the chalice nobody could decide afterwards, but drop the chalice he did with a clatter. Dan saw it falling and, helpful as ever, made a dive for it, collided with Father Tierney and sent him hurtling down the steps towards the altar rail. He tried to rise but his foot became entangled in his cincture and he went down again with the thump of a stricken hunter.

The sight of the writhing priest was too much for Dan. He panicked, vaulted the altar rail and made for the door. But when some of the men left their pews to aid the priest Dan thought they were about to attack him, so he wheeled, vaulted the altar rail again and took off like a hare through the sacristy and out of the church, heading for the grave-yard, his surplice flapping behind him like a spinnaker.

Father Tierney had already had his grave dug, a fine deep grave with the sides all nicely smoothed, and into this Dan leaped, and there he stayed until dark.

It was a pity that Father Tierney had taken it into his head to visit his grave in the evenings. There was nothing morbid about these visits. He was, he told himself, simply familiarising himself with his last resting place.

That evening, a crisp one but bright enough, he made his way to the grave, the events of the morning long gone from his mind. Dan heard his footsteps and crouched lower in the grave, trying to freeze as he'd seen threatened animals do. But like those animals he could contain himself for only so long, and as the footsteps got closer, louder and more menacing, he began to shake uncontrollably. And the shaking scared him more, and it was the fright of it all that made him hurtle from the grave and flee into the night.

'Something not right about it,' was the verdict. 'Not right going and dying like that in your grave before you're dead.'

'And the face on him? Will you ever forget it? Like he'd seen the devil himself.'

'And being down there three days before Fergal found him.'

'We don't know it was three days.'

'Must've been.'

'It comes from digging your grave before you're ready for it, and that's a fact. Tempting providence.'

'No worse than getting your plot.'

'That's different. Man's got to have his plot. But getting it dug and ready while there's breath in your body, that's asking for something to befall you.'

'It was the fright that killed him.'

'What fright?'

'The fright of falling in, of course. What fright did you think I meant?'

'That fright the looney Loftus gave him in the morning.'

'Oh.'

And they started to think about that and weigh it up like they were looking for someone to blame as though to absolve Father Tierney of tempting providence. The way their dull minds worked it wasn't long before they were nodding into their beer and saying, yes, it was probably that looney Loftus who had been responsible, upsetting the priest the way he did.

By the Tuesday they were all agreed: Dan Loftus and his manic ways had made the priest collapse into his grave. And from then on they stopped thinking of Dan as a harmless idiot. They began to hate him and think him dangerous, and there was anger in their voices when he was mentioned.

The bishop, with time on his hands, came to Father Tierney's funeral. So did all the villagers. So did Dan. He didn't go into the church for the ceremony but waited patiently by the grave until they carried out the flower-bedecked coffin.

Freddy Carson was the first to spot him, and he muttered to Jim Quail out of the corner of his mouth, 'That fucking maniac is there.'

'Jesus,' said Jim. 'What do we do?'

'Run him off,' said Freddy.

'I dunno,' said Jim, fearful that running anyone off holy ground might get the Almighty upset.

But Freddy had no such qualms. A stupid man, he was delighted to be able to bully someone stupider than himself. 'I'm shifting him anyway,' he said. 'You please yourself,' he added and started towards Dan.

Jim Quail was still uncertain. 'What's Freddy up to?' someone asked him.

'Gone to run Dan Loftus off from the grave.'

'Better help him,' the someone said. 'Come on, Jim.'

And in the manner of such things others joined in. Soon there was quite a band of them, eleven at least, marching towards Dan, getting there in time to hear Freddy say, 'You're not wanted here, Loftus.'

Dan stared at the men, puzzled.

'Go on. Get yourself off before we throw you out.'

Still Dan stared.

'You goin' or not?'

Dan smiled, but it was a tentative smile, nervous and jittery, which looked mocking. Freddy didn't like that. He wasn't going to be made a fool of in front of everyone. On impulse he kicked out, sending his boot fiercely into Dan's crutch. Dan doubled up in pain, and that started things. They all decided to have a go at kicking and thumping him while the cortège paused and the bishop, at the back, enquired what the delay was and thought that a glass of dry sherry would go down nicely.

Later, alone, Dan nursed his wounds, putting a paste made from dock leaves on the cuts which covered his face and wincing as he applied the salve. He winced too when he walked, because his testicles were badly swollen and there was pain and a funny noise in one of his knees. Gingerly he lowered himself to the floor and sat there, his legs drawn up, his arms about them, and brooded. He knew his body had been hurt. He knew his feelings had also been hurt but he couldn't have explained why. And there was something different about him, something inside him had changed. Although he could never have put a tag on it, a viciousness had started to consume him. Wounded, he wanted now to wound. And as he sat there and the day drifted into night he plotted, and his plottings were terrible since there was no part of his mind set aside to control them.

14

They said much the same thing about Freddy Carson as they had about Father Tierney. 'Did you see the face on him!' they said. 'Will you ever forget it? Like he'd seen the devil himself.'

'Any of you seen my Freddy?' Mrs Carson wanted to know.

'Uh-huh,' the small group said.

'Well if you do tell him to get home this instant, will you?'

'Yes, Mrs Carson.' And then, 'Treats him like he was a child, she does, instead of nearly thirty.'

'Funny though we haven't seen him.'

'Yeah. It is a bit.'

'Haven't seen him for – it must be three days, I suppose.'

'Me neither.'

'Funny.'

'Yeah.'

'Not like him to go off like that and not leave word behind. Specially with his Ma.'

'No. T'aint.'

'Wonder where he's got to?'

The Morrissey brothers found out where he'd got to although they wished they hadn't. 'Shittin' Jesus,' Phil Morrissey said. 'It was awful. Really bloody awful.'

'Sure was,' his brother Finbar agreed. 'Bloody awful.'

'Never seed anything like it in my life.'

'Nor me.'

'For Christ's sake will you tell us about it and not go on saying how bloody awful it was.'

'I'm coming to it,' Phil said, relishing his moment of attention. 'I'm coming to it. Just hold your whisht . . .' He took a deep, long swig of beer and smacked his lips. 'Aaaaah,' he said. 'Where was I now? Oh, yes. Well, Finbar and me was coming home, normal like, through the woods, and Finbar said to me what's that in Christ's name. So I looked and there was this kind of funny thing lying on the ground. We didn't know what it was at first, did we, Finbar?'

'No, we surely didn't.'

'Will you get on with it!'

'I'm getting on with it. Like I said this thing was lying on the ground so we had a closer look. And Jesus, if it wasn't Freddy. Dead to the world. And his neck caught in one of those jaw-traps he liked to set for foxes and the like. Almost taken his head clear off, it had. You could see he'd been trying to get the trap open 'cause two of his nails were almost out and nothing but blood on his hands.'

'How the hell would he get his neck in it?'

'You tell me. But his neck was in it and that's for sure, and the eyes of him popping out of their sockets.'

'Must've been drunk.'

'Maybe.'

'Drunk and fell over.'

'Maybe.'

'Bang with his head and snap with the trap. Could've happened.'

'Maybe?'

'Did he smell of it? Drink?'

'Didn't sniff him. Wasn't going to get that close to his face. Jesus God, it was every colour of the rainbow.'

'*Must've* been drunk.'

'Maybe.'

'What else would have made him put his stupid neck in the trap?'

Phil Morrissey shrugged, and his brother followed suit like his actions were controlled by his brother at the end of an invisible wire. 'Nothing else, I s'pose.'

'Well then. Must have been the drink.'

It was as well for Dan Loftus that they supposed nothing else, although they could hardly be blamed for not so doing. They couldn't have been expected to, and certainly not to blame Dan, who had vanished almost eight weeks earlier, two days after he had taken the terrible beating at Father Tierney's funeral. Nobody missed him at first but only because nobody was that anxious to see him. Still, after a fortnight had passed they started remarking on his absence. 'Haven't seen that fool Loftus these past weeks. You?'

'Naw. Don't want to either.'

'Funny though.'

'S'pose it is.'

Finally, Matty Bruton, who had always coveted Dan's farm and had an eye to acquiring it, said the police should be told. So the police were told, and they went to the farm and poked into everything and found nothing.

'Ain't been lived in for Christ knows how long,' one of them said.

'Not right having a good farm like that lying deserted and fallow,' Matty Bruton said.

'You're right there.'

'Maybe he's dead,' Matty Bruton suggested hopefully.

'Aye. Maybe he is and all,' the policeman agreed with a twinkle.

'So the farm would be sold, eh?'

'Could be that's right too, Mr Bruton. Have to find the body first though. Nobody's dead without their dead body to prove it.'

But Dan was far from dead. Like any prey which had survived he had simply gone into hiding, gone to higher ground as it were, abandoned the farm and built himself a shack in the woods with timber and corrugated iron transported from the farm at dead of night. And he made it quite comfortable, more comfortable than the cold, stone farmhouse had been at any rate, and covered the hut with branches of evergreen softwoods, disguising its existence cleverly. He ate well, snaring rabbits for one thing, and making forays into the village when darkness fell and returning with vegetables, and sometimes a chicken or meat or a pie left hanging outside in a timber-and-mesh safe by some unsuspecting housewife. Cunningly, he never lit a fire, eating everything raw, so the pies and cold cooked meats he filched were a special treat. And it was while he was checking his snares that he spotted Freddy Carson doing the rounds of his traps.

There was something furtive about Freddy as he moved from trap to trap. Following him, Dan was overcome by a sense of hunting, the more so since he was being very silent, bending and twisting to avoid low-hanging branches, side-stepping twigs with the agility of an Indian. The fact that Freddy was oblivious of his presence heightened the feeling of a chase, and before long Dan was enjoying himself. More, he was thrilled. His heart thumped, and each time he stopped he could feel his nerves quivering. He noticed how silent it had become: not a sound from animal or bird. It was as if they were on his side, keeping still so he could hear every move that Freddy made.

Freddy bent down and dragged the dead fox from the trap, and something told Dan that now was the moment to confront him. As Freddy straightened, looking pleased, smiling, his teeth yellower than those of his victim, he saw Dan. Instantly, he froze. His entire body froze – his smile, even his strands of thin wheat-coloured hair, which had been ruffling in the light breeze. Dan took a step nearer and Freddy defrosted.

'What you doin' here, Dan?' he asked, repeating the question immediately as the words croaked unintelligibly from his throat. 'What you doin' here, Dan?'

Dan said nothing.

Freddy started to back away.

Dan followed.

'You keep off of me,' Freddy warned.

Dan just kept advancing.

'I'm tellin' you. Keep off of me.'

Dan, almost playfully, stamped his foot.

Freedy, still walking backwards, tripped on a root and tumbled on to his buttocks.

God alone knows why but that triggered something in Dan's mind, and he was on Freddy like a shot, sitting astride him, his weight alone holding the skinny man down. He took the fox and laid it gently to one side, Freddy releasing it without a murmur. Then he took Freddy by the wrists, rose, and began to drag him back towards the trap. It was then that Freddy started to scream, a weird, unmelodic cry like a lovelorn vixen which echoed through the woods. A magpie wickedly took up the cry, imitating it at first, then cackling, mocking the perpetrator. Other birds, small ones, suddenly appeared on branches for a closer look, cocking their heads perkily, twittering pleasurably among themselves.

Dan turned Freddy on to his back and placed his knee between his shoulders. He prised the trap open, setting it again expertly. Then he cupped his hand under Freddy's chin and dragged his head between the steel jaws. Freddy screamed again.

Dan stroked his head, consoling his victim.

The traps snapped shut with a terrible, delicate click.

Freddy tried to scream again, but only gurgled.

Dan stood beside him, staring down, watching the slow

process of death, nodding as if he were beginning to understand that mystery.

Freddy reached up with both hands and tried to lever the trap open.

Dan placed a foot on the steel, pressing.

Freddy scrabbled away uselessly with his hands.

Dan watched.

Freddy's eyes started to pop out of their sockets.

Still Dan watched unmoved.

Finally, Freddy shuddered and died.

Dan took the dead fox back with him to the shack. He laid it on the floor and poured himself a drink, smacking his lips as the strange concoction made of wild sloes and strawberries burned his gums. Then he buried the fox, giving it a decent burial, putting leaves over its eyes so the dirt wouldn't get into them, and pulling the lips down over the bared fangs to give the fox a better aspect when it resurrected.

15

Of course it couldn't go on for ever: Dan hiding in the woods and never being seen. Molly Morris, whose constipation had been giving her a lot of trouble, spotted him as she squatted on the cracked bowl of her outdoor lavatory. The sight of him skulking through her garden at dead of night with a small, bulging sack over his shoulder fair frightened the life out of her, but it cured her constipation which was something.

'I'm telling you, Peggy, it was him,' she told Peggy Walshe next morning as they both hung out their washing, using the one line since that was more practical.

'Ach, you imagined it, Molly.'

'I did *not*,' Molly insisted, getting peeved.

'Sure, he's been gone from here this ages.'

'Well, he's back, I tell you, if he ever went away.'

'I hear Molly Morris saw Dan Loftus th'other night.'

'So I hear.'

'You think she did?'

'She says she did.'

'Yea, but d'you think she really did?'

'She's not given much to imagining.'

'That's what I mean. It *could* have been him.'

'Sure it could.'

'Well, where's he been then all this time?'

'Huh. God knows.'

'*I* thought he was dead.'

'Maybe he is.'

'Shit! What's that supposed to mean?'

'Maybe she saw his ghost. Ever think of that?'

'Haw! That's a good one! You and your ghosts.'

And although it was certainly meant as a joke, the impression lingered, and soon others were saying things like, 'You know, if he *is* dead it could have been his ghost.'

Then Bert and Angela Ennis saw him so the ghost theory was abandoned, or almost. Dan still remained shadowy and spectral in their minds, and this made him greatly feared, capable of committing any atrocity. So, when Jim Quail was found with his own hunting knife plunged into his heart rumours abounded that Dan Loftus had done it. Of course, some admitted, Jim *could* have just slipped and fallen on the knife, I mean, it *could* happen, couldn't it? And if it had happened like that they wouldn't have an excuse for going after Dan, would they?

'It's revenge he's after,' Mr Biddlecombe decided. 'Them's the two who beat him up at the priest's funeral.'

'There were others,' someone pointed out, and suddenly they were all looking at each other speculating who might be the next to die mysteriously.

'He'd never do that,' Joe Connolly said, putting words to their thoughts.

'Wouldn't bank on that.'

'Jesus. You think he would?'

'He's made a start, hasn't he? Who's to say where he intends to stop.'

'But sure we were all there.'

'That's right.'

'He can't kill all of us.'

'Can't he?'

'Of course he can't.'

'He can bloody try.'

'Jesus! We better get him before he gets us then.'

But try as they might they could not find Dan or the shack he had built. Several people saw him, certainly, but only when they were by themselves and there was no way they would tackle him under those circumstances.

So the spring passed, and the summer passed, and autumn came, and the enthusiasm for hunting down Dan Loftus lost impetus because nobody else was killed or died in anything but an ordinary way. And the men found themselves mocking themselves, wondering aloud over beer how they could have been so stupid to imagine that daft Dan had anything to do with the deaths of Freddy Carson and Jim Quail. 'Just coincidence', Mr Biddlecombe said, and the men nodded, even those who didn't know what coincidence meant.

Dan, in an odd way, was sorry they had stopped trying to find him. He enjoyed outwitting them even though it had meant staying well clear of the village and harsh deprivation through lack of proper food. Still, with winter now well on its way again, and the long hours of darkness to conceal him, he could venture back to the village and nourish himself properly.

16

Mr Biddlecombe's shop was quiet as a morgue. Only the occasional sniffle broke the silence as watery snot was sucked back into rheumy nostrils. Once someone coughed and everyone jumped and glared at the cougher for making them reveal their fear.

Mrs Biddlecombe clicked her needles ferociously.

'So much for coincidence,' Matt Dillon said finally.

Mr Biddlecombe ignored what might have been a slight.

'Was Phil one of them?'

'One of who?'

'One of the ones who – '

'Beat Dan? Can't remember. Doubt it. Phil wouldn't have hurt no one.'

'He was,' Mr Biddlecombe put in, putting the glasses he had polished on a thin ledge over the bar. 'I saw him. I remember. Landed a hefty kick or two, I recall.'

They were talking about Phil Meacher, the postman, who'd been found that morning with his postbag tied over his head, well dead from suffocation, and his face the colour of the uniform he was supposed to wear but seldom did – not unless there was a telegram to be delivered, or maybe at Christmas.

'You're all of you jumping ahead of yourselves,' old Mr Fergison now said, his two walking sticks hanging on the bar in front of him and his buttocks on the lowish stool which by tacit agreement had become his. 'Who's to say it was Dan that did this one – or the others for that matter. Just looking for someone to blame, you all are, just so you won't be blamed yourselves.'

That made them think a while, for Mr Fergison never said much so when he did his words were embalmed in a certain ancient importance.

'Nobody else'd do such things,' Matt Dillon dared.

'Oh wouldn't they?' Mr Fergison asked.

'No. Why should they?'

'Why should Dan Loftus?'

'Because – '

'Because you've given him some daft reason for doing it,' Mr Fergison interrupted. 'That's the only reason.'

Which really set the cat among the pigeons, and for a couple of weeks everyone was looking at everyone else and wondering if they had a reason for the killings; and there was a lot of whispering going on; and people remembered old grievances and differences like how so and so had been expecting dollars in a letter from a cousin in America which never arrived and hadn't he suggested that Phil Meacher might have pocketed them? And hadn't Freddy Carson been the one who told Des Kegan he was an impotent old sod and offered to service his wife for him and hadn't she, out of the blue, come into child, and hadn't that made them all snigger and made Des look a right sort of moron? And hadn't there been that to-do between Jim Quail and Austin Flynn about the ram that was supposed to be the horniest thing on four legs and turned out to be useless after Austin had paid a small fortune for it? And what about, and wasn't, and hadn't, and didn't they say – so it went, dredging up fictions long since forgotten, and twisting them a bit, and in the twisting making them sinister and fit reasons for dreadful revenge, and causing Mr Biddlecombe no end of worry since business was dropping off with nobody coming for a drink in case he found himself boycotted by the others and with the possibility of murder lumped on his shoulders.

99

'It's got to stop.'

That's what the new priest, Father Devlin, said from the pulpit, possibly in case they stopped attending church as well as the pub. But what he said made little difference, although everyone agreed he was right.

'It's not up to any of us to have even suspicions,' Father Devlin went on. 'It's up to the gardai to prove who did it,' and he stressed the word 'prove'.

But the gardai were as baffled as everyone, and they weren't that interested anyway, not wanting to hike all the way from the town to the godforsaken village and take statements and listen to the rantings of a load of simpletons. And, of course, when they too couldn't find Dan they put *that* down to 'just rustic skitterings' as Sergeant Bullock entered it in his report which got around in the mysterious way that such things do get around, and made the villagers furious, and made them shut their mouths whenever the police asked them anything.

So, on the morning they found Andrew Gillsenon tied to Matt Dillon's Hereford bull and him hardly recognisable after being dragged about the field and trampled on all night, they decided to say nothing to the police, and their secrecy drew them together again, and the togetherness made them less suspicious of one another, and the old grievances were tucked away again for another day.

'We'll deal with this ourselves,' Matt Dillon said, still worried that the ordeal might have done something untoward to his bull.

They all nodded.

And then, without anyone mentioning his name, without anyone actually saying anything, it was agreed, mutely and finally, that Dan Loftus must be found, and killed, and his corpse handed over to the gardai, and then they could all get back to the business of living out what was left of their lives.

*

'They're going to kill Dan.'

'Shush, boy,' said Mam, like everyone else not wanting to talk about it now that the decision had been irrevocably made.

'I like Dan,' I said, trying that as a defence for him.

'Shush,' said Mam again.

'It's not fair.'

'It's none of our business. And what would you know about fair and not fair and you not out of short trousers yet?'

'I like him,' I said again.

'Like him or not you keep well out of the way.'

'Don't you think we should help him?'

'Who? Dan Loftus? Is it out of your mind you are?' Mam asked looking aghast, then adding with a small note of triumph and relief, 'Anyway, we don't know where he is.'

Poor Mam. If she'd known she'd have dropped dead there and then even before she got round to the washing up. I knew where Dan was. I'd known for months. And Dan knew that I knew, but he didn't seem to mind. He never spoke to me or anything but he didn't chase me away or seem hostile, which was the same as him speaking to me, I suppose.

'And he might be dead already for all we know,' Mam was saying, like she was almost hoping he was.

'Yeah, he might,' I answered. 'Probably is.'

'Well, then. There you are.'

'Yeah.'

There I was all right: standing brazen as you like agreeing with everything Mam said, and all the while I was thinking what I could do to protect old Dan, even imagining smuggling him into the house and up to my room and putting him under the bed where I hid everything I didn't want Mam to see.

'There!' Mam said. 'The sink's full. You wash yourself and get to bed.'

'Now?'

'Now. Getting far too uppity you are, my lad.' Then she came across and cuddled me. 'But you're the best boy in the world, aren't you?'

''Course I am.'

Mam laughed at that, and went on laughing and shaking her head at my cheek while I washed in the sink and dried myself with the big white towel that had been nicely warmed up by the range.

Alone in bed I said to Dan, 'Don't worry', and I said to God, 'Help me to look after Dan,' and I said to Dan again, 'Don't worry. God's going to help us.'

BOOK THREE

17

It came to that time of year when Dan found himself feeling lonely. The time of year when antlers clashed as warring stags sorted out their territories while doe-eyed does grazed uninterestedly; the time when vixens screamed their urgent need for a mate; the time when young girls bridled and became young women and ruined themselves by slapping on their faces the trappings of womanhood, and boys became men and sniffed the exotic bottled scents, stripping the girls with their eyes as they minced by, some even stealing the frilly underwear from clotheslines and snuggling up to it at night.

However this year, for Dan, there was something different about his need, and a terrible instinct took hold of him. He set his sights on Kitty Daley.

'You were dreaming, girl,' Mrs Daley told her daughter. And later, 'I wish they'd hurry up and find that Dan Loftus,' Mrs Daley said to Mrs Biddlecombe. 'He's preying on everyone's mind. Kitty thought she saw him in her bedroom last night, would you believe.'

'Fiddlesticks,' said Mrs Biddlecombe, using the word her mother had always used, and her grandmother too.

'I told her she'd been dreaming,' Mrs Daley countered defensively.

Mrs Biddlecombe kept on knitting but peered over the top of her spectacles. She mouthed the word 'fiddlesticks', but didn't utter it aloud in case it made her lose count of her stitches.

'You don't think he could have, do you? Come into her room like she said?' Mrs Daley asked.

Mrs Biddlecombe sniffed, but said nothing.

Mrs Daley persisted. 'What do you think I should do?'

Mrs Biddlecombe put her knitting down with a sigh. 'Take the girl to sleep in your room,' she suggested logically.

'I suppose,' Mrs Daley supposed, although it was clear she didn't think much of the idea. It occurred to her that it might encourage Dan Loftus to come into *her* room, and that would certainly be worse than his visiting her daughter's.

'That way Gleb could shoot him if he came. He can shoot, can't he?'

'Gleb? Of course he can shoot,' Mrs Daley said, instantly defending any suggested shortcoming in her husband. 'It'd be waking him up that would be the problem. A terrible sleeper he is. Nothing wakes him.'

'Well, *you* could shoot him,' Mrs Biddlecombe said logically.

'Me?'

'Yes. You.'

'I couldn't do that, Mrs Biddlecombe.'

'Why not?' Mrs Biddlecombe snapped, all this talk making her irritable.

'I just couldn't.'

'Heard the latest?' Matt Dillon asked, and looked peeved when the two men nodded. 'What do you think?'

Tom Bell shrugged. 'Could be true,' he said.

Peadar Felim nodded. 'Could be,' he said.

'What was he wanting? That's what we should be asking,' Tom Bell said.

'What d'you think he was after?' Matt Dillon said, scoffing. 'Only one thing he could have been after.'

'With Kitty?' Tom Bell sounded amazed. 'Sure she's the ugliest thing God ever put together,'

'That wouldn't worry him. It wouldn't be her face he'd be hankering,' said Peader.

'Maybe the old fool doesn't see her ugliness,' Matt Dillon said, and in a way he was right.

The ugly face and slim pale body of Kitty Daley haunted Dan. He was consumed with passion for her. He kept remembering that people had always called Kitty Daley the ugliest thing on two feet, and he wanted to rescue her from that. He wanted to tell her she was pretty. He wanted to make a fuss of her and look after her. But most of all he wanted to penetrate her, and he thought about that all day and long into the night, seeing himself on top of her, runting away time after time after time. And as he heard the antlers clash and the vixen howl, he howled inside himself, the gorgeous pain in his loins making him shudder and groan.

There was a huge bright moon. Slivers of cloud speckled it, making it look like a globe of the earth. The farmhouse stood out clearly, with Dan standing in the yard. The windows had been boarded up, and the door padlocked. Matty Bruton had seen to that, masking his hoped-for acquisition behind charity. 'He's bound to have relations who'll be wanting his place. Everyone has relatives when they die,' he added when he saw the funny look they gave him.

Dan smiled to himself. He saw the boarded windows and the padlocked door as just another part of the villagers' plan to harass him. He loped across the yard and went into the cow byre. He stopped and sniffed, and for a moment looked quizzical, cocking his head like he was trying to remember something special. He groped his way along the wall, making for the dark, far end of the byre. He said *Yup* when he came to the small door which led from the byre to the pantry where the hams and Deirdre had hung, and put his shoulder to it. It opened about a foot and then stuck. Dan squeezed through. He stood there, quite still, listening. Then he shook himself like a horse, from the neck down, and began scampering about the house. Upstairs he went, into what had been Deirdre's and her mother's bedroom. One corner of the ceiling had collapsed and the floorboards under it were already rotting. But the bed in the other corner was dry. He grabbed the horsehair mattress and hauled it downstairs to the pantry. Then upstairs he went again, rooting in the cupboard on the landing, yanking out what blankets had not been sold off at the auction. They were damp and mouldy, as was the old eiderdown, its feathers congealed into lumps. An old bolster caught his eye, and he took that too. A bunch of lavender, tied with a wide pink ribbon, fell to the floor. he gathered it up, sniffed at it, smiled, and added it to his collection.

Back in the windowless pantry he settled the mattress midway between the doors and covered it with the blankets and eiderdown, placing the bolster carefully at the head. He found a jam-jar and put the lavender in it. Then he looked about. Satisfied, he locked the door leading from the pantry to the kitchen, locked it from inside and put the key on the ledge over it. He locked the door from the pantry to the byre too, but this key he put in his pocket. He seemed happy and lightfooted as he made his way across the yard. He didn't look back; he kept his head down and chatted away to himself like someone with great plans afoot.

'Been back, has he?' Matt Dillon asked Mrs Daley as their paths crossed outside Biddlecombe's shop. She was leaving, he going in.

'Who?' Mrs Daley asked, pretending not to know. She hadn't much enjoyed the fun that had been made of her, and she knew the men were saying she'd be lucky if mad Dan did take that ugsome daughter off her hands.

'Dan Loftus, of course.'

'No he hasn't,' Mrs Daley snapped, and flounced off, her big bottom like a bustle behind her.

'Women!' Matt Dillon exclaimed to Mr Biddlecombe, and Mr Biddlecombe nodded in the manner of a man who understood perfectly what he meant. 'Always bloody imagining things,' Matt added. 'Do anything to grab the attention, they would.'

Mr Biddlecombe nodded again.

'Like I said before, she should be grateful if old Dan *did* have a go at Kitty. It'd be the only time the girl would have it.'

Mr Biddlecombe liked that and grinned with his yellow teeth. 'You're right there,' he said.

18

Mrs Daley's screams woke the whole village. Lights snapped on and windows and doors were flung open, with heads popping from the one and bodies appearing in the other.

'He's taken her,' Mrs Daley screamed. 'Oh, my God. Oh, my God, he's taken her,' she screamed, her hair, usually constrained in a tight bun at the nape of her neck, flying about her face, her flannel nightdress billowing in the night breeze.

'Taken who?' someone called. 'Who's that making all the rumpus?' the same voice wanted to know. 'What's going on?'

Gleb Daley, dazed and still half asleep, wandered on to the street, saw his wife 'displaying herself', as he saw it, made a grab for her and started pulling her back towards their house. 'Will you come in off the road, woman,' he told her. 'And stop making a show of yourself.'

'She's gone,' Mrs Daley wailed.

'Who's gone?' Matt Dillon asked, taking charge as usual.

'Kitty. Our Kitty,' Mrs Daley said. 'That Dan Loftus came and took her from under our very noses.'

'What's she talking about Gleb?'

'She's saying Dan Loftus took Kitty,' Gleb said.

'I know what she said,' Matt said. 'Is it true?'

Gleb Daley shrugged. 'She says it is.'

'It is,' Mrs Daley insisted. 'I saw him, I tell you. Running off across that back field with Kitty thrown over his shoulder like a sack of spuds.'

'Better get her inside and give her a cup of tea, Gleb,' Matt said. 'When she's calmed a bit we'll try to get sense out of her.'

Gleb looked alarmed at the prospect of having to make tea.

'Molly,' Matt called to Molly Donleavy. 'Would you ever go with them and make a pot of tea to quieten her down?'

Later, despite being calm, Mrs Daley stuck to her story. She had seen Dan Loftus abduct her daughter and cart her off over his shoulder like a sack of potatoes.

Later still Mr Biddlecombe opened his shop so the men could have beer and talk the matter over. There was none of the tension which had followed the earlier killings. Somehow the abduction of Kitty Daley was so unlikely that it was funny.

'It proves one thing, if we didn't know it already,' Larry Cunningham said. 'Dan Loftus *is* mad. To be taking Kitty Daley he must be out of his mind.'

'We better organise ourselves and go look for her,' Matt Dillon said, but seemed in no great hurry.

'Aye,' the men chorused, and sipped their beers.

'We'll split into four groups,' Matt said.

The men nodded. 'Whatever you say, Matt.'

'We can cover the woods from the four points then,' Matt explained.

The men nodded sagely.

'From the north, south, east and west.'

'That's right,' Larry Cunningham put in as though that had been in his mind all the while.

Mr Biddlecombe wasn't so sure. 'What happens if he's not in the woods though?'

'Of course he's in the woods,' Matt Dillon insisted. 'Where else would he be?'

Mr Biddlecombe shrugged and turned away. He hadn't expected to be asked that.

Gleb Daley came in, looking the worse for wear. 'She says I'm not to come home 'till we've found Kitty,' he said gloomily. 'And she means it, damn her.'

'Comes from lettin' her have her own way too long, Gleb,' Bobby Sinclair said with feeling, being in much the same position himself.

'I 'spose,' Gleb agreed resignedly.

'We've just been organising ourselves,' Matt Dillon said. 'You better come along.'

Gleb nodded dismally. 'Aye. Better.' Then a thought struck him which was rare. 'What happens if we don't find her?'

'We'll get you a tent, Gleb,' Bobby Sinclair said, and they all had a good laugh at that.

'Taking the dogs?' Mr Biddlecombe enquired.

'Too many traps about,' Matt Dillon told him. 'Freddy Carson, God rest his soul, had them all over the bloody place. Can't risk losing a good dog,' he added. Not for Kitty Daley at any rate, he thought.

'Not for Kitty Daley at any rate,' Larry Cunningham whispered in Matt Dillon's ear, making him jump hearing his own thoughts jump back at him like that.

'Mind how you go, men,' Mr Biddlecombe said as he watched them form themselves into their little groups and set off down the road with lanterns carried in front and behind. One or two raised a hand to acknowledge his benediction but they didn't bother to look round, just waved their hands with a bit of a flick at the wrist.

'I'll never knit another stitch if those morons find Dan,' Mrs Biddlecombe said to her husband as he came back into the shop, shutting the door behind him and locking it, and pushing the bolts across for good measure.

'If he's to be found they'll find him,' Mr Biddlecombe

replied, slipping the tape of his striped apron over his head, sticking up loyally for the menfolk.

'Couldn't find their faces if they weren't stuck to the front of their heads,' Mrs Biddlecombe maintained.

'They'll find him. And Kitty,' Mr Biddlecombe insisted.

'We'll see,' Mrs Biddlecombe said, plaining and purling away for all she was worth.

It was well past dawn and teeming down when the men straggled back to the village – cold and wet and miserable and, most of all, angry. They stood, huddled, by the war memorial, stomping their feet and flicking their heads to keep the rain out of their eyes.

'Waste of time that was,' Larry Cunningham said.

'Surely was,' someone agreed.

'Should have waited 'til light,' someone else pointed out. 'Whose idea was it anyway to have us tramping through the woods in the middle of the night?'

Heads turned and stared at Matt Dillon.

Matt Dillon glared back.

'Oh,' said the voice that had asked the question.

'Let's go home and dry out,' Matt Dillon said.

'Best idea I've heard in a while.'

'What about Kitty?'

'What about her?'

'Well – we just leaving her?'

'We'll look for her again. This afternoon, maybe.'

'Might be too late, that.'

'If he's going to do anything to her he'll have done it by now. Few more hours ain't goin' to make a gnat of a differ.'

And they did try again in the afternoon.

By dusk they had trooped home again, miserable and forlorn and hangdog.

'What did I tell you?' Mrs Biddlecombe asked smugly

as her husband filled the glasses and tankards with pale beer and porter and gave her a filthy look. 'Couldn't find their faces if they weren't stuck to the front of their great thick heads,' she added triumphantly.

'Not a bloody sign of them,' Matt Dillon revealed after downing half his beer. 'If they're in the woods they're underground or somewhere.'

'Did you look everywhere?' Mr Biddlecombe asked, trying desperately to salvage something which would restore his faith in them.

'Everywhere,' Matt Dillon said.

'And not a sign?'

'Not a sign. Jesus, he covers his tracks well, does that fool.'

'Too clever for you by half,' Mrs Biddlecombe said, mostly to her husband, who ignored her. 'And would you listen to that halfwit calling Dan Loftus a fool!'

'You'll be trying again tomorrow, won't you?' Mr Biddlecombe asked.

' 'S'pose we'll have to,' Matt Dillon said.

Mrs Biddlecombe cackled away to herself.

'You're bound to find him tomorrow,' Mr Biddlecombe encouraged.

'Huh,' grunted Mrs Biddlescombe.

'Maybe,' said Matt Dillon.

'Course you will,' said Mr Biddlescombe.

'Huh,' grunted Mrs Biddlecombe again, and Mr Biddlecombe gave her a look that said he'd throttle her if she grunted once more.

'All very well finding him,' Marty Heever put in. 'But will youse be able to catch him?'

Nobody answered that, perhaps wondering what Marty Heever was on about, and waiting for him to expand on it.

'Looking at how you've done so far I'm thinking I'd have a better chance of catching him myself,' Marty expanded, which was a terrible insult.

Marty Heever had only one leg; he'd lost his left one by getting it caught in a rotary saw he was operating, although he never explained what he'd been doing with his leg that high up. But he'd been fond of his leg, and when he came back from the hospital on crutches he bought his burial plot, and had the severed leg buried with some ceremony, erecting a little gravestone to its memory. HERE LIES MY LEG THAT I'LL BE ALONG TO JOIN SOON, it said. And as if that wasn't enough he visited the grave every day to reassure his limb that he'd meant what he'd written.

'Maybe we should – ' Bobby Sinclair began.

'Should what?' Matt Dillon demanded, irked by Marty and rounding on Sinclair.

'Nothing,' said Bobby, wilting.

'Where's Gleb?' Mr Biddlecombe asked, noticing that Gleb Daley was missing, and using his absence to clear the air.

'Ha!' exclaimed Matt Dillon. 'Gone to try and make the peace with herself.'

'And if she's any sense she'll stick to her word and leave the eejit locked out for the night,' Mrs Biddlecombe muttered.

19

Dan Loftus sat cross-legged on the floor and stared at Kitty Daley. It had been quite a struggle to get her to the house for she was a great weight and had fought him all the way, and now he was tired. She'd stopped fighting now, and it was very quiet in the pantry. Peaceful, Dan thought. Like it should be.

Kitty Daley had been asleep and naked when he'd taken her, and she was still naked now lying on the mattress, although Dan had thrown his old overcoat over her loins. But she was wide awake, her small eyes bulging in their sockets. She'd stopped struggling for there was little point in it. Her hands were secured behind her back, her legs were tied at the ankles, and there was a rag in her mouth, held by a length of bailing twine tied neatly behind her neck. Her long black hair spilled over the bolster and she looked comfortable enough, so Dan just sat there looking at her. She was frightened of him, he knew, but that would pass, he told himself. Might take a day or two but it would pass. When they got to know each other she'd be right as rain. Like every trapped creature she was scared, but she'd come to trust him. He'd give her all the time in the world to do that. And then she'd be tame and get to like him, and they'd get on like a house on fire.

Kitty groaned. Instantly Dan was beside her, stroking her hair. 'Shush now,' he whispered. 'Shush now.'

The candle he'd lit sputtered, and the wax hissed softly. Dan reached out and brought the candle close to Kitty's face. Kitty groaned again, rolling her eyes. She looked a bit blue in the face but maybe that was the candlelight. A spot of hot wax dripped on to her cheek and she gave a muffled scream.

Dan put the candle on the floor, taking his time, letting wax form a nest before setting the candle on it. Then he removed the wax from Kitty's face with great care and gentleness, using the tip of his finger. He leaned over and kissed the spot. 'That'll take the pain away,' he told her. It was the longest speech he'd made to anyone since the day of Father Tierney's funeral.

Dawn was chipping away at the darkness when Dan decided to remove the gag from Kitty's mouth. 'There,' he said. 'That's better, isn't it?'

'Water,' Kitty pleaded, her swollen tongue making the word unrecognisable. Dan looked puzzled.

'Water,' Kitty said again.

'Oh,' said Dan. 'Water.'

He hadn't thought about that. Or about food either; that was something he picked up for himself as he needed it. The idea of stocking up would never have entered his head. Now, 'Water,' he said again. 'OK.'

He re-gagged Kitty and left the cellar by the byre, locking the door behind him. He decided to take a chance and go back into the village to see what he could find. A chicken would be nice. Kitty would like chicken, he was sure.

Wisely, he took a circuitous route, approaching the village from the west. He could just pick out the lights which still shone in Biddlecombe's store, and he thought he could hear people speaking even at that distance. It was the best part of twenty-four hours since he'd taken Kitty, and he noticed he was peckish enough himself. He raised his head and sniffed the air. Then he moved rapidly, crouching as he went, down to the village, making for

Matt Dillon's house because Mrs Dillon always had a bucket under the leak in the gutter to catch the rainwater she used for washing her special blouses and slips. Besides, Mrs Dillon kept chickens and ducks and a few geese, and sold their eggs despite not needing the money.

As he approached the fowl house the birds began to move about, clucking and squawking and stamping on the roosts. Dan froze, letting them settle down. Then he moved on, making little clucking noises himself. They seemed to work: the fowls remained quiet. He unlatched the thin wooden door of the shed, and grabbed the first thing his hands rested on. A plump white goose. He strangled it there and then, twisting its neck and breaking it before the bird had a chance to protest. He tucked it under his arm. Next he went around the side of the house. A light was on in one of the rooms, and shone out on to the narrow concrete path. Dan bent low and passed beneath the window. He had to grope to find the handle of the bucket, but he found it all right. He was just straightening up when the back door opened and Mrs Dillon stepped out.

For what seemed an extraordinarily long time the two of them stared at each other, both with their mouths open, both transfixed. Then Mrs Dillon let a bellow out of her, and Dan took off, clutching the goose and the bucket.

The devil got into Dan. He'd only run maybe three hundred yards when he stopped. He set the bucket of water carefully on the ground, and the goose beside it. Then he squatted on his hunkers and watched to see what would happen.

He didn't wait long. Mrs Dillon was out of the house as soon as she'd put shoes on instead of slippers, and was storming off towards Biddlecombe's. Dan chuckled gleefully. He trotted back to the Dillon house and crept into the kitchen. Over the range, running the whole length of the room, were wooden slats on pullies, and from them dangled Mrs Dillon's washing. Dan eyed it. He unhooked the rope from the clasp set in the wall and lowered the slats. He walked carefully down its length, touching each garment. There was a pretty nightdress, white with pink flowers on it and an embroidered collar, so he took that. And a pair of knickers. and some socks for himself. Mrs Dillon's shopping basket was on the chair nearby. He put the clothes in it, and threaded his arm through the handles. There was a tin of peaches on the table, open, so he popped that into the basket as well, ignoring the syrup that spilled over everything. He took a spoon and a fork and a knife. He went back to the clothes rack. A pair of woollen mittens and a striped shirt were added to his trove.

Even from inside the Dillon house he could hear the commotion at Biddlecombe's, and he decided enough was enough. He loped off, collected the goose and the water and made his way back to the farm, thrilled with his booty.

Mrs Dillon put her formidable weight against the door and burst into Mr Biddlecombe's store. She stood in the doorway, seething, glancing about for her husband. When she spotted him she made for him like a crazed bullock. She swiped at him, sending his beer glass flying across the bar. 'A fine specimen you are, and no getting away from it,' she roared. 'You in here guzzling away and that Dan Loftus down at your own house stealing my geese.'

'Shit,' said Matt. 'Come on, lads.'

Mrs Biddlecombe gave a hoot like an owl.

'No good your going now,' Mrs Dillon snapped. 'He's well gone.'

'We're going,' Matt insisted.

'Better we wait an hour,' Bobby Sinclair opined. 'Be light enough then. Don't want to be tackling him in the dark, do we?'

'You're right,' said Matt. 'Shit Jesus. No sleep again.'

'And no sleep at all until I get my goose back. And my bucket,' Mrs Dillon shrieked.

'I'll get your goose and bucket, woman.'

'See that you do.'

Mrs Biddlecombe fair doubled herself up with sniggering.

Rather than being frightened by his encounter with Mrs Dillon, Dan thought of it as fun. He chuckled to himself as he made his way back to the farmhouse. At the gate into the yard he stopped, placing the bucket, now only half full of water, and the shopping basket by the post. He wheeled away from the farm, trotting back the way he had come, but veering off into the woods before he reached the village. Once in the woods he began to pluck the goose, purposely dropping the feathers in small clumps along the trail, saying, as he dropped them, one for Matt and one for Bobby and one for Tom, and one for everyone he could think of – having the time of his life. In a clearing he set about cleaning the bird, severing its head with his hunting knife and yanking out its intestines, leaving them in a pile for the fox. That done, he peered through the trees at the sky. Nearly dawn but misty, which was good. He gathered twigs and dry moss and lit a fire, lighting it with some matches. Then he piled bigger wood on top, getting the fire going really well. As he waited for the heat to intensify he found a nice length of willow and rammed it through the goose. Holding one end in each hand he rotated it like a spit until he considered the goose was cooked. Then he stamped out the fire thoroughly, and trotted off down the hill, back to the farm.

'Hey,' Bobby called. 'Hey, Matt. Over here.'

'Feathers,' Matt observed. He bent and felt them. 'Goddam goose feathers too.'

'That's what I thought,' Bobby said.

'Whistle the others up, Bob.'

Bobby put two fingers into his mouth and sent a shrill whistle through the woods.

When they had all gathered, Matt said, 'Silly bugger's gone and left a trail. Knew he'd slip up some time.'

'Silly bugger,' someone repeated.

'Let's get after him then,' Matt said, and they set off in single file, following the feathers.

'Made fools of you again, did he?' Mrs Biddlecombe wanted to know.

'Just got away afore we could catch up,' Matt explained.

'We'll catch him tomorrow,' Bobby Sinclair said. 'Like Matt said, he's made his first mistake.'

'Mistake,' Mrs Biddlecombe scoffed. 'Mistake indeed! If you ask me he *wanted* you to follow those feathers. Oh, he made right fools out of you and no mistake.'

'He wouldn't have the brains to do that,' Matt decided.

'More brains than the lot of you put together he has,' Mrs Biddlecombe said.

'We found his fire,' Bobby tried.

'Of course you found his fire. You were meant to find his fire,' Mrs Biddlecombe said. 'He's led you a merry dance again.'

'Here,' Dan said, offering Kitty a drink. He had tossed the lavender out of the jam-jar and filled it with water, and now held the jar to her lips. Kitty drank deeply, gulping and spilling some of the water on to her chest. Dan wiped it carefully with his hand. 'Feeling better?' he asked. Kitty nodded.

'Got us some food too,' Dan told her. 'You like goose?' Kitty nodded again.

Dan began to carve the goose with his knife, slicing it nice and thin for Kitty, big thick chunks for himself. The bird was very greasy and both of them made slurping noises as they devoured it. Dan fed Kitty piece by piece and gently wiped the grease from her lips with a filthy handkerchief.

When they'd had enough, Dan cut another length of twine from the roll he'd used to tie Kitty. He bound the goose's legs, made a loop and hung the bird from one of the hooks in the ceiling. 'Have some more later,' he told Kitty amiably.

'I want to go home,' Kitty said.

Dan gave her a baleful look.

'Why'd you bring me here?'

Dan kept looking at her.

'I'm frightened.'

Dan softened his look and gave her an encouraging smile.

Kitty started to struggle with her bonds.

Dan went on looking, pleased and proud that his tyings with stood her efforts to escape.

Then Kitty started to cry.

And Dan got very upset.

Kitty wept and snuffled.

Dan came across and sat on the mattress beside her. He pulled out his dirty handkerchief again and wiped away her tears. 'Don't cry,' he told her. 'Don't cry.'

'I'm frightened,' Kitty told him again.

'No need to be,' Dan assured her. 'I'll look after you.'

'I don't want you to look after me. I want to go home.'

'This is your home now,' Dan told her, and there was a firmness in his voice which frightened her even more but calmed her too in an odd sort of way.

Mrs Daley gave the men two more days to find Kitty, and when they failed she took matters into her own hands and went to the gardai.

'Two days and a bit?' the Sergeant asked. 'Sure that's

not missing, Missus,' he told her. 'Has to be gone a week or more before we'd call it missing in these parts.'

'She was kidnapped,' Mrs Daley said, shuddering at the mere mention of the word but none the less enjoying the important sound of it.

The garda looked doubtful. 'Kidnapped, you say?'

'Yes. Kidnapped.'

'And why would that be? Why would anyone kidnap your daughter?'

'To – I don't know,' Mrs Daley snapped, knowing all right but not about to say it in case it besmirched her daughter's reputation.

'You don't know?'

'No.'

'And it was a Dan Loftus, you say, who kidnapped her?'

'Yes.'

'You saw him?'

'Yes.'

'He walked into your house and carried her off?'

'Yes.'

'And she didn't scream or anything?'

'Well – no.'

The garda gave a deep sigh, and used the tail end of that sigh to make his question sceptical. 'You wouldn't think, would you, that your daughter, maybe – just maybe, mind – ran off with this Dan Loftus?' Mrs Daley gave him a withering glare.

'No. Well, you should know, I suppose.' The Sergeant gave another huge sigh. 'If I was you, Missus, I'd give it another day or two and see if she turns up. If she hasn't come home by the end of the week or got in touch with you, we'll come out and have a look.'

'She could be dead by then.'

The garda clicked his tongue against his teeth and muttered something about not looking on the gloomy side until there was something to be gloomy about.

'They're as bad as that lot of eejits,' Mrs Biddlecombe said when Mrs Daley told her what had transpired at the garda station. 'But he was right about one thing. No point in looking on the gloomy side yet.'

'I can't help wondering what he's doing to her,' Mrs Daley moaned.

Mrs Biddlecombe gave her a look over her spectacles which suggested only a halfwit couldn't imagine what he was doing to her. But she said, 'Don't be thinking about that sort of thing at all. Letting your mind run off with you.'

But Mrs Daley couldn't prevent her mind from running off with her. It was one of the more pleasurable things about the kidnapping. Starved of sex by a husband who had long since lost interest, and too proper or afraid to dally outside the home, Mrs Daley imagined incredibly lurid goings-on between Kitty and Dan and, lying in bed next to her snoring husband from whom she'd inevitably lifted the ban, she kind of wished they were happening to her.

She'd have been disappointed. There was nothing erotic going on between Dan and Kitty. True, Dan would lie beside Kitty at night and put an arm about her, but that was as far as it went. Certainly he wanted to do more but he abstained, waiting, he told himself for the right time.

20

The goose lasted them four days. Dan didn't eat much himself; privation through the years had shrunk his stomach, so he gave most of the bird to Kitty. At the end of four days, though, Kitty was sick of it. 'Can't you get something else to eat?' she asked.

Dan nodded. 'What?'

'Anything but goose,' Kitty told him.

'Rabbit?'

Kitty wrinked her nose. 'No.' she said. 'Not rabbit.' she thought for a bit. 'Mutton,' she said finally. 'I'd like mutton.'

'Right,' Dan told her, and determined to find her some mutton. He was pleased she made this demand of him. She was calming down as he had known she would, and although she was still fettered a curious bond had grown between them. Kitty no longer held her breath when he lay down beside her in the night. Indeed, she snuggled closer to him. And her eyes no longer held any terror. Instead there was a strange yearning in them, a pleading she had never had the chance to show to any other man. Dan saw this new glimmer and recognised it, and used it to stimulate himself while away from the farmhouse, telling himself he must save Kitty for a special time. It was like, he remembered, his father breaking a wayward filly. 'Not yet, Dan,' his Dad had said when Dan had urged him to mount the animal. 'Not yet. She may seem broke and amenable, but that's the time when all the damage can be done. There's still the smell of fear from her no matter how placid she seems. When that smell goes, then I'll mount her. Not before.'

And Dan, as he lay beside her at night, could still catch that whiff of fear from Kitty.

Matt Dillon's dog whimpered like it was afraid of something. The hairs on its back bristled and it lunged at its chain.

'What's the matter with that dog?' Young Frank asked his Dad.

'Time of year,' Matt told him, not wanting to get up from the fire and take a look.

'What d'you mean time of year, Dad?'

'You'll know when you're older,' Matt told him.

Outside, the dog gave a fearsome howl, and then started barking furiously.

'Goddammit,' Matt swore and got to his feet.

'Want me to go?' Young Frank asked.

'No, I'm up now.'

Matt Dillon went to the door and peered out. 'What's the matter with you, Billy?' he asked the dog.

The dog grudgingly wagged its tail and whimpered again.

'Something out there?'

The dog yapped.

'Shit,' Matt said and went indoors to get his gun. 'Something bothering him all right,' he told Young Frank, and loaded the gun.

'I'm coming too.'

They stood together in silence for a few minutes, listening to the sounds of the night. 'Better unchain him and see where he goes,' Matt said. Young Frank unchained the dog.

Released, Billy took off across the yard, vaulted the gate and sped out towards the fields.

'Let's get after him,' Matt said.

At the stile they paused and listened again. Nothing. Matt whistled. Away in the lower field Billy barked once.

'He's with the sheep,' Young Frank said.

The full moon gleamed, and an owl flew across it, its shadow making the two men duck. 'Shit,' said Matt, and they both chuckled. Now they could hear Billy whining. 'Shit,' said Matt again. 'Something's happened down there.'

By the time they got to the sheep field they were out of breath, panting hard. Billy had rounded up the flock, leaving them in one corner, and was lying by something, guarding it. Matt cocked his gun, and the two of them walked slowly towards the dog.

'Jesus Christ!' Young Frank swore. 'Them roving dogs been in again.'

Matt shook his head. 'No dog done that,' he said.

'You'd have to see it to believe it,' Matt Dillon told Mr Biddlecombe and the rest of the men in the shop. 'Perfect. Done like a butcher. All that was left was the skin and that taken from the carcass as neat and as tidy as you'd wish.'

'And the guts,' Young Frank pointed out.

'And the guts,' Matt agreed. 'Whoever done it cleaned the beast out and all. Took their time about it too, you could tell.'

'That's right,' Young Frank said. 'Took away the heart and the liver and the kidneys.'

Sounds like someone knew what they were doing,' Mr Biddlecombe said.

'Knew what they were doing all right,' Matt echoed.

'Got to eat, hasn't he?' Mrs Biddlecombe put in.

They all stared at her.

'Him and Kitty, if he's still got her. Kitty Daley. And Dan,' she said. 'Thought I smelled something cooking during the night.'

'Why didn't you say something, woman?' Mr Biddle-combe demanded.

'Because in the first place I didn't know a sheep had been stolen. And in the second what business is it of an old woman like me to tell you great men what's going on?'

They found the fire over which the ewe had been roasted. It was two miles from the one that had cooked the goose; four miles from Dan's farm.

'He's moved north,' Tom Bell said.

'Maybe that's what he *wants* us to think,' Matt Dillon replied.

'He wouldn't think devious,' Tom Bell thought aloud.

'Maybe not.'

'Wouldn't have the wits.'

'Expect you're right.'

'Sure I'm right.'

They all moved north, spreading out in a line, their eyes to the forest floor in search of clues.

'Not sight nor sign of him. Or Kitty Daley,' Matt Dillon confessed later. Mr Biddlecombe shook his head in bewilderment. 'You'd think there'd be some sign of them, wouldn't you?'

'Why would you?' Mrs Biddlecombe put in, enjoying herself again. 'He has you all running around in circles and he's laughing his head off at ye.'

'Be quiet, woman,' Mr Biddlecombe snapped testily.

Mrs Biddlecombe opened her mouth but changed her mind and stayed quiet. But she smiled broadly, and her needles clicked a bit louder, and her eyes twinkled in secret delight. It was a long time since Mrs Biddlecombe had enjoyed herself so much.

The smell of roasted ewe filled the pantry. Dan hung it on a hook, and smiled at Kitty. 'Mutton,' he explained. 'Back soon,' he added.

The side of his face and his hands and his clothes were bloody from the carcass. By the stream he stripped naked, not seeming to notice the cold, and washed himself, scooping water into his hands and splashing it all over his body. Then he washed his clothes. Well, he dunked them in the water and tinted the water pink. He didn't bother to squeeze them dry, just flung them over his shoulder and went home, letting them drip along the way.

Back in the pantry with the door locked safely behind him, he hung his clothes on other hooks, and then, still naked, he began to carve the meat. It fell from the bone, pink and tender and still quite warm. He tasted a morsel himself before giving some to Kitty. 'It's good,' he reassured her. 'Try.'

He sat on the mattress beside her and fed her patiently, waiting while she chewed and swallowed before offering her another titbit. In between mouthfuls he gave her water from the jam-jar. It struck him that he'd been foolish to carry that bucket all the way from Mrs Dillon's when there was clean, fresh water running by the farm, and he frowned as he tried to puzzle out why he'd done that. Maybe it was just the bucket he wanted, but he couldn't figure out why he'd want that either. Kitty noticed the frown and looked anxious. But then Dan was smiling at her again, and she relaxed.

When they had finished Dan wiped his hands carefully on the mattress and gleefully pulled Mrs Dillon's shopping basket towards him. He started to unpack, studying each item carefully, almost as though seeing it for the first time. He laid everything on the floor in a line. When he came to the nightdress he held it up and beamed at Kitty. 'For you,' he said.

Oddly, Kitty recoiled. For some reason the thought of the nightdress made her feel more vulnerable than being naked.

'You don't like it,' Dan said flatly.

'I do,' Kitty said nervously. 'It's very nice.'

'Yes,' agreed Dan, but he'd lost interest in it. He dropped it on the floor, and lay down beside Kitty. The smell of fear had left her.

'We'll just have to try again tomorrow, and keep trying 'til we find him,' Matt Dillon said.

'No point in trying tomorrow,' Mrs Biddlecombe said, ignoring her husband's glare. 'They've enough food now to last them an age. Far better you spend the time getting what rest you can and organising yourselves properly.'

'She could be right, you know,' Mr Biddlecombe said grudgingly.

'Could be,' Matt Dillon conceded.

The other men nodded, the thought of rest pleasing them.

'Of course I'm right. What you need is one or two of you to stay up all night, every night, and keep an eye out for him when the food runs out. He'll be back again then.'

'Makes sense,' Mr Biddlecombe allowed.

So that was what they decided to do. They'd organise themselves into posses of two and take it in turns to patrol the village at night. Being very cunning about it of course. That way they'd surely catch Dan when he came back to replenish his stock.

'It was clever of you to think of that,' Mr Biddlecombe told Mrs Biddlecombe as they locked up the shop.

Mrs Biddlecombe said nothing. She was delighted with herself. The thought of the fools patrolling the village amused her no end. Something else to giggle at when Dan outwitted them yet again.

Kitty gave a little scream when Dan broke the hymen and penetrated her, but there the distress ended. As Dan wriggled and grunted about on top of her, Kitty grunted and sighed beneath him. For nearly thirty years she had waited for this, dreaming about it, her dull mind running riot and conjuring up unimaginable delights. But it was better than anything she had dreamed. Her tongue sought out all the crevices on Dan's face, darting in and out of his mouth like an adder's, into and out of his ears too. Her loins writhed and heaved as she pushed herself harder against Dan, and between sighs she kept whispering, 'Harder, harder, harder.' And when their orgasm finally exploded, in unison, she wrenched a sound from herself the like of which Dan had never heard before except from a bull in anger.

Dan didn't withdraw. All night they lay like that, and all through the night they runted, and each time Kitty cried, 'Harder, Dan, harder,' and each time she gave her bull's bellow, and each time something inside her careered about in joy.

'He's picking on you, Matt,' Mr Biddlecombe said flatly. 'First tying poor Andy Gillsenon, God rest his soul, to your best Hereford, and now making off with your ewe.'

Matt Dillon remained unusually quiet.

Then Tom Bell, fool that he was, had to say, 'And maybe it'll be yourself next.'

Matty Bruton, still with his eye on the farm, said, 'We've got to *do* something about it.'

Matt Dillon nodded. 'Yeah. But what?'

'We've tried everything,' Tom Bell said.

'He'll be back,' Mrs Biddlecombe predicted from her high chair. 'Ten days now since anything's happened. Can't be much of that ewe left. He'll be back, mark my words.'

'Who's on tonight?'

'We are,' Phil Morrissey said. 'Me and him,' he added, jerking his glass towards his brother.

'Well, mind you stay awake.'

'Don't none of you worry. If he comes within a mile of us we'll have him for sure.'

'Unless he gets you first,' Mrs Biddlecombe had to say, and the men all stared at her with loathing. She'd been right up to now, hadn't she?

21

'Untie me, Dan,' Kitty said in a wheedly voice.

Dan eyed her.

'I'm getting terrible sores on my wrists and ankles,' Kitty told him.

Dan studied her ankles and then rolled her over on her stomach and examined her wrists. They were rubbed raw and bleeding, fresh blood on top of congealed blood. 'You'll run,' Dan said.

'I won't. Honest I won't,' Kitty promised.

Dan compromised. 'I'll free the hands,' he said, and freed them.

Kitty swung her legs off the mattress and sat there studying her bloody wrists. Then, without warning, she started to cry.

'Don't,' Dan said, and patted her head.

'They hurt,' Kitty told him between heavy sobs.

'Here,' Dan said, and took her hands in his. He bent his head and started to lick the wounds. His rough tongue removed the fresh blood and the old congealed blood. 'There,' he said, smiling.

Perhaps it was the taste of the blood that made Dan realise he was hungry. 'You hungry?' he asked.

Kitty nodded.

'I'll get something. Not now. At dark.'

And at dark Dan got ready to go and find food. But he tied Kitty's wrists again before he left and ignored her tears, and didn't think to ask her what she wanted.

The brittle, frosty night air crackled about his face as

he left the farmyard and made for the village, hugging the leafless hedgerow, bent double. The heavy smell of burning peat in the fires and ranges of the houses made him feel colder, and he stopped for a while to jump about and flap his arms to keep the circulation going. An old dog fox, also on the hunt for sustenance, watched him without fear: it drew back its lips and showed its teeth in a kind of wretched smile. An owl flew past, wheeled, and came back for another look, then silently wheeled away again. The fox watched the owl and licked its chops, then gave his full attention to Dan and his antics, and kept his eye on him as Dan set off down the lane again.

On the outskirts of the village, near Jim Porter's smithy, Dan stopped again and cocked his head. He had heard, he thought, voices. Two of them. Two men. Talking in low tones they didn't want to be overheard. Dan moved slowly forward. He saw the Morrissey brothers leaning against the memorial to some long-forgotten heroes, smoking, smoking just the one cigarette, passing it between them, each taking a suck and passing it back. Dan grinned mischievously. Quietly he shuffled his feet, felt what he wanted, and bent to pick up the stone. He hurled it across the road. It clattered on to the rubbish dump, striking a can or some old corrugated iron.

'Jeez, what was that?' Phil Morrissey asked.

'Shit if I know,' his brother said, stubbing out the cigarette on the memorial.

Dan threw another stone, this time in the opposite direction. It thudded on to the grassy verge. The two men swung round. They both had rifles and they cocked them simultaneously.

'Can't be in both places,' one of them said.

'Fucker can, you know,' the other answered.

Dan smiled.

'You check out that one and I'll take the dump,' Phil said.

'OK.'

Dan followed Phil to the dump and after a short silent struggle throttled him.

'Phil – ?' Phil's younger brother called. 'Hey, Phil? Anything?'

His voice echoed in the icy air, mutilated sounds waiting for an answer.

Dan was well down the village street by the time he heard the young man calling his brother. He squeezed through a gap in the hawthorn hedge, and crept up to Pat Foley's cottage. There was a light in one window so Dan peered in. Pat and Mary Foley and one of their four children sat comfortably in front of the fire. Pat was reading. Mary Foley was reading too; she seemed to be reading to the child for every so often she would glance up from the book and look at the child, and the child would nod, and Mary Foley, would go on reading again. Dan watched them for several minutes. Then he moved around the side of the cottage to the small wooden shack where Pat Foley stored his vegetables. Pat had a way with vegetables – everything he planted grew. He always had plenty to store since nothing died. And he covered them with sacks so there'd be plenty handy to take them away in. Made good soup, Pat Foley's vegetables did. Make a change from all that meat. The door of the shack scraped on the path because the only hinge that held it was loose. Dan froze and listened.

A dog barked, but that was some way off. He went into the shack and began filling a sack with vegetables. He had to do everything by touch, but he knew what he was doing, selecting parsnips and carrots, potatoes and a swede or two, onions, beetroot and a sweet mangel. The sack was soon full, as full as he could manage to carry anyway, and he set off, the sack over his shoulder. He had trouble manoeuvring it through the hedge: he had to back out, pulling it after him. He had just managed to swing the sack back on to his shoulder when he felt the barrel of the rifle on his cheek.

'Don't you move an inch, Dan Loftus,' the young Morrissey said. 'Don't even breathe.'

Dan didn't breathe.

'You done throttled my brother, you bastard. Christ Jesus, just you wait 'til we're done with you.'

In a single economical movement Dan bent his knees, twirled the sack off his back, and clouted young Morrissey squarely on the shoulder, sending him reeling and his rifle spinning on to the road. Then he was off, running like a hare, the sack abandoned on the roadside. He heard the boy bellow behind him and kept running. He thought he heard the rifle being cocked again and kept running. He felt the bullet rip into his shoulder, like someone tapping him for attention, and kept running. The next bullet missed him, zinging past his ear, but the explosion of the rifle sounded like it was just behind him, and he kept running.

BOOK FOUR

22

'Help me!'

It was one of those April days that sometimes come inexplicably after a bitterly cold snap: warm and bright and blue, when there shouldn't have been any pain or hurt about. But the cry was filled with pain, and when it came, unexpectedly from nowhere, it made the hairs stand up on the nape of my neck and sent goose-pimples bubbling on my arms. It sounded so forlorn there in the woods, and I remember the trees were deadly still like they were chilled by it too.

'Help me!'

I couldn't see anyone. I squinted and looked about. It wasn't even a voice I recognised, very soft and plaintive like a woman's. I tried to call out, 'Who's there', or something like that, but the words stuck in my gullet, and I just croaked.

'Help me!'

I coughed, and called, 'Who's there?' loudly, feeling braver at the familiar sound of my own voice, squeaky though it was, on the point of breaking, warbly as though I had a cold.

'Me. Over here, boy.'

'Where? I can't see.'

'I see you. Over here. Just come on straight.'

I kept on straight, but slowly, like Red Indians did, and every time a twig snapped under my feet it sounded like gunfire and made me wince. Then I saw Dan. An old oak had fallen, tearing half its roots from the ground, and Dan was lying under it, not trapped just hiding.

It was ages since I'd seen him. Four or five weeks anyway. Not since he'd taken Kitty Daley away from her bed. I'd looked for him, and gone to the little hide he'd made in the woods, but even on the first visit I knew he'd abandoned it. It had an air of loneliness about it that could only have come from abandonment. You feel it in old houses once the dwellers have gone, but only in houses that have been special.

In a way I couldn't explain, I'd missed seeing Dan. My meeting him was my only real secret, and at that age you need secrets to survive. And, as Mam said, he was in huge trouble now, abducting a woman from her bed.

'He's in huge trouble now,' Mam said to her sister, Aunty Hilary, who was visiting for a couple of days and sat agog as Mam told her of the goings-on in the village, saying, 'My, oh my', and 'Fancy that now', to keep Mam going, and looking very pleased when Mam said, 'Oh, you don't know the half of it,' and leaning forward in her chair, her little eyes bright as a sparrow, waiting to hear the half she didn't know about.

'Your hand, boy,' Dan said, holding out one of his own.

I took his hand and helped him up: it was huge and rough and horny. The other hand was covered in dry blood and hung by his side like it was useless and withered.

'How long you been here?' I asked.

Dan thought for a while. 'Dunno,' he said finally. 'Since this,' he added, indicating his left shoulder.

'Since Morrissey shot you?'

'S'pose,' said Dan.

'He *did* hit you then?'

Dan looked at me as if I was stupid.

Nobody had believed Morrissey. They thought he'd run away and left his brother to be killed. I'd sit outside Biddlecombe's and listen to them talk. It was nice and warm out there since Mr Biddlecombe had an outdoor brazier for cooking hams and he kept it burning. It smoked a lot, but the spicy smoke seemed warm too. Besides, I could surreptitiously smoke a cigarette butt and nobody knew the difference.

'What d'you mean you saw nothing?' Matt Dillon demanded.

'Like I said. I saw nothing. Just heard something. Two things. Rattles or something. Phil went to look at one and I went to the other, and when I got back I found Phil dead.'

'And then what?'

'I was coming back to get help and I met him – bumped into him – coming out of Foley's garden with this sack on his back.'

'Then what?' Matt Dillon persisted.

'Then he hit me with the sack and ran off.'

'I thought you said you shot him?'

'I did.'

'Huh.'

'I shot *at* him anyway. Don't know if I hit him but I think I did.'

'Huh.'

'It's true. Every word of it. You saw the sack.'

'That's all we saw.'

'Maybe we'll find the body in the morning,' Morrissey said hopefully.

'Maybe,' Mrs Biddlecombe said doubtfully.

But they didn't. Looked everywhere but found nothing, so they didn't believe Morrissey's story, and didn't bother to look for Dan any more for a while.

'We're all getting jittery,' was the way Mr Biddlecombe put it. 'Seeing things that ain't there.'

'Where you living Dan?' I asked.

'Home,' Dan told me.

'Home?'

'The farm.'

141

'The farm?'

'The farm. My farm.'

'Jeez,' I said, amazed.

'Help me get there, boy.'

'OK.'

It took us a long time to get to the farm. Dan was pretty weak, and I wasn't much help to him. He wouldn't let me into the house with him, but said thank-you politely. He didn't ask me to say nothing. I suppose he knew he didn't have to.

I was nearly home myself when I noticed all the blood on my shirt – Dan's blood. 'Jeez,' I said to myself, using that word since it made me feel grown up and I was too scared to say Jesus as a swear. I took off my shirt and ripped it where the blood was. Then I broke a bit of old thorny bramble from the hedge and jiggered it across my shoulder holding one end in each hand. It hurt pretty bad but it brought the blood up well.

'What have you done to yourself?' Mam demanded.

'Huh?' I said.

'Look at your shirt.'

'Where?'

'There. And your shoulder all ripped.'

'Must have caught it in something, Mam.'

'Of course you caught it in something. Was it wire?'

'Dunno.'

'If 'twas wire and the wire was rusty God alone knows what you'll get.'

'Don't think it was wire.'

'I'm taking no chances.'

Mam took the shirt off my back and washed the blood away from my skin. Then she made me bend over and poured iodine on to the cuts. That hurt worse than the bramble. 'Mam!' I protested.

'Be quiet,' Mam snapped, and poured some more. 'Maybe that'll teach you to be more careful.'

Later, when we'd eaten and were just sitting there waiting for the time to come so we could go to bed, I asked, 'Any more about Dan?'

'Dan?' Mam repeated, then narrowed her eyes. 'Why d'you ask that?'

I shrugged. 'Just wondered.'

'Well, don't you bother your head wondering about him.'

'They still waiting for him?'

'I hear so.'

'D'you think they'll ever get him?'

'They'll get him. One day.'

'You sure, Mam?'

'No, I'm not sure. Only one thing is sure and that's that it's time you were in bed, young man.'

'Aw, Mam.'

'Bed.'

'Yes, Mam.'

'Kiss me first.'

I kissed Mam like I did every night after she told me to, on the cheek.

'Sleep well.'

'I will.'

I didn't.

The next day was Thursday, and Thursday was the day Mam did her baking. She made lots of loaves, enough to last us for the week and a few over to give to the old women who could no longer find the strength to knead the dough. I never thought she counted them but she did.

'That's strange,' Mam said.

'What is, Mam?'

'Seems to be missing a loaf.'

'You count them?'

'Of course I count them, silly.'

'Better count them again.'

143

'I did. Must have given it to someone,' Mam said, shaking her head. 'Must be getting old too,' she added, and dismissed the matter, but she gave me a funny look first.

I figured: since Dan had lost his sack of vegetables, and since he'd got no food when I helped him back to the farm, he must be pretty hungry by now.

I tapped on the door of the farmhouse, and whispered, 'Dan, it's me,' but the place remained quiet. I tried looking in the windows, but couldn't see anything that gave a sign of life. I peered into the cow byre. Nothing. I left the loaf, wrapped in newspaper, at the door of the byre since that was where Dan had gone in.

23

'I'm starving,' Kitty moaned, and that was no more than the truth. It was four days since she'd eaten, two while Dan was missing, and two since he'd come back wounded. The days she spent alone were the worst. The bindings cut cruelly into her flesh, and the gag all but choked her, soaking up what little moisture was in her mouth. And she had been forced to foul the mattress, and now sores had developed between her legs. Yet she had been pleased to see Dan again despite his unwillingness to release her, and she offered to tend his wound. But Dan had rejected this, settling for sitting alone in one corner of the pantry, licking the sore that had turned dark blue and was festering. Now, at the sound of Kitty's voice he looked up. He made an effort to stand but toppled back again, giving a small woebegone cry as his damaged shoulder bumped against the wall.

'Stay still,' Kitty told him, since it was the only thing she could think of to say.

'Food,' Dan said.

'You can't do anything about it in the state you are,' Kitty said. Then: 'If you'd untie me I could get us something to eat.'

Perhaps Dan was considering this, or perhaps he hadn't heard her, but he said nothing, just put his head between his knees and sat there, snuffling or giving low, phlegm-filled coughs from time to time.

Once, Kitty thought she heard someone tapping at the door at the front of the house and considered crying out for help. Then the tapping sounded on one of the windows so she supposed it was the ivy in the wind, and did nothing, lying quite still since movement pained.

'This is getting beyond a joke,' Mam said.

'What is, Mam?'

'First a loaf vanishes into thin air, and now the last of that vegetable pie has gone.'

'The cat?' I suggested, innocently as I could make it.

'Cats don't eat vegetables.'

'Yes, they do.'

'No, they don't. And don't argue with me.'

'Oh. I remember. I ate it.'

'*You* ate it? When? Why didn't you tell me?'

'Yes. Last night. I was hungry. Forgot to tell you. Sorry, Mam.'

Mam didn't believe a word of it, but she said, 'Well, that's all right then. Tell me in future.'

'Yes, Mam. Sorry.'

Then she said, 'Did you eat the loaf too?'

'Oh no, Mam,' I told her truthfully.

'Oh,' Mam said, like she was disappointed at not solving the entire mystery.

I wondered if Dan had taken the bread and pie. The bread had still been where I left it when I took him the pie. God, I said, when I was tucked up in bed, please make Dan find the food I left for him, and make him better. And then I went to sleep feeling better since God never let anyone down.

'I'm beginning to think maybe Morrissey did kill him,' Matt Dillon said.

'What makes you say that?' Mr Biddlecombe asked.

'Well, been more'n a week now and nothing else's happened.'

Mr Biddlecombe shrugged as if he didn't take much to that argument.

'Won't ever believe that 'til I see the body,' Tom Bell said.

'Maybe he's just lying out there wounded,' Mr Fergison said, coming in with his canes, like someone on four legs, and overhearing.

'Sufferin',' Tom Bell added.

'That's a thought,' Matt Dillon said, and they all latched on to that, and enjoyed it for the rest of the evening.

I took four eggs to the farm. The other food, the bread and the pie were still there, and it struck me that maybe Dan had died. Maybe he was right there in the cow barn dead. I went in to take a look. Well, he certainly wasn't in the barn. Then I heard the moan. It seemed to come from inside the wall. It came again. I went deeper into the barn, and came to the little door. I knocked on it. 'You in there Dan?' I said in a loud whisper. Someone moaned again from behind the door.

It had one of those handles that you put your hand into and turn. I did that, and pushed. The door opened. Light from the byre flooded in but it took me a while to get used to the murkiness.

Kitty Daley was lying on a mattress on the floor. She was very still. Her mouth was open, and her skin looked dry and was a funny colour, green almost. I could tell it wasn't her that had moaned. Dan was crouched in the corner. He was a funny colour too, but he was breathing, and what I had thought were moans was his breath rasping from him.

'Hey, Dan. It's me.'

Dan didn't move.

I went over and touched him. Just touched him.

Dan toppled over.

'Jeez,' I said to myself.

I sat down beside him and cradled his head in my lap. He blinked at me and seemed to smile. 'You'll be fine,' I told him. 'Brought you some eggs. Want one?'

Dan made no reply but I took it to mean yes. I tapped an egg on the flag floor. Then I opened Dan's mouth and let the yolk and white stuff flow in. Dan gagged, but then swallowed. I did the same with the other two eggs. 'There you go,' I told him. 'That'll keep you going. I'll bring some milk tomorrow. Milk's good for everything.'

I knew Dan needed more than milk and eggs, and all the way home I argued with myself, one bit of me saying I should tell Mam about Kitty being dead and Dan being sick so she could get a doctor, but the other bit kept telling me if I did that I wouldn't have Dan to myself any more. I said nothing to Mam.

'You heard what Matty Bruton's been and done?' Mr Biddlecombe asked, looking pompous now that he had something to tell that no one else knew.

'No. What?'

'Only got himself permission to take over Dan's farm, that's all.'

'From who?'

'Ain't heard. Land Commission or something I suppose. Courts maybe.'

'Trust him.'

'Oh, trust him is right. Great what a bit of money will get for you.'

'Matty Bruton's taking over Dan's farm,' I told Mam in dismay.

'Mr Bruton to you, lad. So?'

'He can't do that. It's Dan's.'

'Dan doesn't have need of it, does he? Not right to leave good land going to waste.'

148

'But Dan might want it later.'

Mam looked at me in her strange way, the way she did when she knew I was trying to say something else. But she said, 'I don't think Dan will be wanting it ever again.'

'You mean they won't let him have it.'

God, I said, can't You keep that Matty Bruton away from Dan's farm, please? They'll find Dan and then they'll skelp the living daylights out of him for sure.

'I want a word with you, young man,' Mam said, catching me just as I was going out the door. I didn't dare turn around or she'd see the bulge under my pullover. I just stopped in my tracks, with the door open, waiting, after saying, 'Yes, Mam?' as innocently as I could make it sound, which wasn't very.

'Look at me when I speak to you,' Mam said.

I had to turn around then unless I wanted a clip on the ear.

'What's that you have hidden there?' Mam demanded.

'Where?'

Mam grimaced at my futile stupidity. 'Under your pullover. Take it out and let me see, whatever it is.'

'Oh *that*,' I said, and took the lemonade bottle half-filled with milk from under my oxter.

'And where do you think you're going with that?'

'Just out.'

'Just out, eh?'

'Uh-huh.'

'And the milk?'

I shrugged, racking my brains.

'I'm waiting,' Mam said, taking a stance, her hands on her hips, like she would wait the rest of the evening and night if necessary.

'For the hedgehogs,' I tried.

'The hedgehogs.'

'That's right, Mam.'

149

'And since when have you become so interested in hedgehogs?'

I squirmed. 'Since the teacher started telling us about them,' I lied.

'Since the teacher started telling you about them,' Mam repeated.

'Yes.'

'I see. Well, that's very nice, I'm sure,' Mam said with one of her looks, and then, suddenly, she turned away and got on with folding the clothes she'd washed in the afternoon.

I started out the door.

'Don't be late,' Mam said.

'I won't.'

'And don't leave that bottle lying around for someone to cut themselves on if it gets broken.'

'I won't.'

Dan hadn't moved, or if he had he had managed to get back to exactly the same position he'd been in when I last saw him. I cradled his head in my lap again, and fed him the milk, giving him only a little at a time so he wouldn't choke. When it was all gone he thanked me with his eyes.

'You've got to get out of here, Dan,' I said. 'Matty Bruton's got the farm now and he'll be coming any time to start working it.'

Dan blinked.

'I'll help you.'

Dan blinked again.

'Can you stand?'

Dan didn't try.

'Come on, Dan. You've got to get out of here.'

'No,' said Dan.

'You've *got* to,' I told him.

'No,' was what Dan said again, and closed his eyes.

*

'Feed your hedgehogs then?'

'Yes, Mam.'

'And the bottle?'

'Oh. I'm sorry. I forgot it.'

'I told you not to.'

'I'll get it tomorrow.'

'Mind you do.'

'Yes, Mam. Sorry.'

God, I prayed, putting a lot of fervour into it, God, please help Dan to get the strength to get out of there before Matty Bruton takes over his farm and finds him. Thank you.

Dan Loftus tried very hard to straighten things out in his befuddled mind. Instinctively he knew that life was slipping away from him, but he didn't regret that. It was all part of that process he did understand. But he was worried what would become of Kitty if he died, unaware that life had long since left her.

He dragged himself across the floor to the mattress. 'Kitty,' he called softly. When she didn't answer he dragged himself away again, thinking she was asleep, thinking he'd untie her tomorrow and send her away. He settled back in his corner.

24

'Sit down,' Mam ordered, and I knew I was for it.

I sat.

'You and me are going to have a talk,' Mam said, which meant, usually, that she was going to talk and I was going to listen. But not this time. 'I want the truth out of you this time. It was you who took that loaf of bread, wasn't it?'

'Yes, Mam.'

'Look at me when I speak.'

I looked at her. 'Yes, Mam,' I said again.

'And you took that and the pie to Dan Loftus, didn't you?'

'Yes, Mam.'

'And the milk?'

'Yes, Mam.'

'What else?'

'Eggs.'

'Eggs?' Mam said, and then smiled. 'I didn't miss the eggs.'

'Only a few.'

'Well, at least we've got that much settled. Now, I want you to tell me where Dan is.'

'I can't do that, Mam. You'll tell the others and they'll kill him for sure.'

'No, they won't. Dan needs help. He's a very sick man.'

'I know that. But he's getting better. Really he is.'

'I don't mean that sort of sick, son.' Mam knelt down in front of me and took my hand in hers. 'He's not well in his mind. He needs help and attention.'

'He's my friend, Mam.'

'I know he's your friend. That's why *you* should help him by telling me where he is so we can get him properly looked after.'

'They'll take him away then, if they don't kill him.'

'Yes. They'll take him to a special hospital.'

'And I won't be able to see him.'

'Not for a while.' Mam stood up and went to the window. She stood there staring out. 'When did you see him last, son?'

'Last night. With the milk.'

'Was he alone?'

'Yes.'

'Kitty Daley wasn't there?'

'She was there all right. But she's dead.'

'Oh my God,' Mam said, and came back to me again. 'You've *got* to tell me where he is.'

'Can I go and see him first?'

'No. Tell me.'

'I want to see Dan first. I've got to tell *him* that I'm telling you.'

'He'll only run away again, son. And then he'll be in more trouble.'

'He won't run, Mam. He can hardly move. Honest.'

'And if I let you go just once more you'll tell me?'

'Yes.'

'Is that a promise?'

'Yes.'

'Say it.'

'It's a promise.'

Mam stood up.

'Very well. I'll make some soup and you can take that along with you.'

'Thanks, Mam.'

'Only this once, mind.'

'I promised.'

'Yes. I know you did,' Mam said and smiled at me kindly. She knew I never broke my promises.

'I brought soup for you tonight, Dan. Mam made it for you special.'

Dan barely moved, but he swallowed the soup well, and I could see he was enjoying it.

It stank in the pantry now. Kitty in particular. There was a smell from her you could hear, humming like. Like flies only there wasn't any flies.

For ages I sat with Dan's head in my lap, stroking his thin, wispy hair like Mam would stroke mine when she was letting me know she loved me. 'Dan,' I said in a whisper, half hoping he wouldn't hear me. 'Mam made me promise to tell her where you are. She says you need help and attention, and that you'll get that in hospital. I don't want to tell her, Dan, but I've got to now. And I'll see to it that nothing bad happens to you. That's my promise to you. They'll make you better and then you can come back and do the farming again. And I'll come and see you every day. Not in the hospital 'cause that's a bit far, but when you come home. Every single day.'

Dan never moved or said anything.

Maybe he hadn't heard.

But I'd told him anyway.

I settled him down as best I could, and took the old overcoat off Kitty who wasn't needing it, and covered him up. For a moment Dan opened his eyes and said, 'Thank you, Sergei,' and then shut his eyes again, his little raving over.

'I'm sorry, Dan.'

Mam was waiting for me. She didn't jump down my throat and make me tell her right away. She gave me a mug of cocoa and a heel of brown bread with dripping on

154

it. And she waited until I'd finished both before she said anything. 'How is he?' she asked.

'Pretty sick. I think it's Morrissey's bullet that's ailing him.'

'Maybe he'll pull through.'

'Maybe.'

'Where is he, son?'

I looked at Mam but she wouldn't look at me. It was the first time she'd ever avoided my eyes so I knew she was hurting for my hurt. 'He's at his farm.'

'His farm? I thought the men looked there.'

'Round the back. A little room off the cow barn.'

'Oh.'

Mam got up and left the room. In a minute she was back with her shawl about her shoulders, the one she threw on when she was nipping out for only a moment. 'I'm very proud of you, son. I won't be a minute.'

'You going to tell them where Dan is now?'

'Yes.'

'I'm coming too.'

'No.'

'Yes, Mam,' I said, and she knew I meant it, and she looked at me as if with those two words I'd somehow changed in her eyes.

As usual, the men were gathered in Biddlecombe's. They stared at us oddly when we came in since Mam never went there but to do her shopping in the daytime. One or two of the men touched their caps and said, 'Evening, Missus.' Mam went straight to the counter and said to Mr Biddlecombe, 'My boy's just found out where Dan Loftus is.'

You could have heard a feather land. Then all the men were talking at once, shouting at Mam and me, asking, *Where? Tell us where?*

'He's at his farm,' Mam said. 'Has been for weeks.'

'We looked there,' Matt Dillon said.

'Hah,' said Mrs Biddlecombe triumphantly.

'In a small room off the cow barn,' Mam explained.

'Shit,' said Tom Bell, then blushed and said, 'Sorry, Missus.'

'Let's get going,' Matt Dillon said, downing his beer first.

'Now hang on. Hang on,' Mr Biddlecombe shouted. 'This is police matter now.'

The men gawped at him.

'Police matter,' Mr Biddlecombe repeated. 'I'll get Jamie to bike it into the town and get the police. Let them take care of it.'

'He'll be off and gone before them eejits get here,' Matt Dillon protested.

'No, he won't,' Mam said. 'He's very sick. He can't move.'

'Acting. That's what he's doing. Acting. Making fools of us again.'

'He's not acting,' Mam said firmly.

'You seen him too, Missus?'

'No,' Mam admitted. 'But my boy has, and if he says Dan can't move I believe him.'

Matt Dillon guffawed. 'Christ! That Dan could fool the lad easy as fallin' off a log. Fooled us long enough.'

'Hah!' said Mrs Biddlecombe.

'All we want to do is catch him and hold him 'til police come,' Tom Bell pointed out.

'Well,' Mr Biddlecombe hummed. 'Well, all right, but I'm sending Jamie to town just the same.'

'You do that,' Matt Dillon said. 'Send Jamie to town for the police and we'll have Dan Loftus all ready for them when they come.'

'You're a bigger fool than I thought,' Mrs Biddlecombe

156

told her husband. 'You don't think for one minute, do you, that they'll bring Dan back alive and whole?'

'I'm going with them, Mam,' I said, and Mam didn't argue. She looked at me hard and then just nodded, and marched off like she wasn't worried about me any more.

Jamie Biddlecombe passed us on his bike, and waved and waved like it was all great fun. And some of the men waved back and cheered him on his way.

Somehow the word had spread and the women and children came to the doors of the cottages and wished their menfolk luck. And someone called back, 'Be home before you know it'; and a woman's voice answered, 'You take care now'; and the man raised his rifle in the air with both hands, and said, 'I'll be taking care, never fear.'

Dogs used for hunting, but tied up now, howled their hearts out, sensing a chase. They strained at chains and rattled them fearsomely, and howled some more for being left out of the fun.

Once outside the village the men stopped talking. Pad, pad, pad went their boots in the dust, and me trotting along behind them, trying to keep up. A big bright moon shone, and the men's breath showed after a while. Most of them breathed through their mouths for some reason, and it looked as if they were all smoking.

25

It looked very peaceful on the farm. You could see it lying below you as you rounded the bend. Not like a place of tragedy at all. Once the men had the farm in their sights they stopped, and shuffled their feet, waiting for someone to take the lead. Matt Dillon did that. 'Now, quiet, lads,' he said. 'Just follow me, but quiet.'

And quietly they followed him down the hilll and into the farmyard. Then Matt called me. 'Where's this door you were on about, boy?'

'In the barn?' Tom Bell butted in. 'That's what you said.'

'Yes.'

'Better show us,' he said, and let me lead the way.

I couldn't get any words out so I just pointed to the door. Someone shone a torch on it, a big torch that lit up nearly all the barn.

'Ready?' Matt Dillon whispered.

The men nodded.

'You stand well back, boy,' Matt Dillon told me.

I stepped back a little.

'*Well* back,' he said.

I stepped back a bit more.

'Ready?' he asked the men.

Again they nodded.

Then they all piled into the little room.

'I'm sorry, Dan,' I whispered.

And I told Dan again that I was sorry when I got into bed. I talked to him for a long time, ignoring God since God wasn't in my good books.

26

Three policemen arrived, and the one in charge wasn't pleased at all.

'One of youse could be facing murder for this,' he said.

'Murder? Us?' Matty Bruton, who hadn't even been there, asked.

'The man was killed, wasn't he? Shot?'

'Yes. Sure he was. But – '

'There you are,' the policeman pointed out. 'If he was shot someone shot him and that someone could be had for murder in my book.'

'But we *had* to shoot him. He was mad as a rabid dog. If we hadn't killed him he'd have killed us.'

'You all agree with that?'

The men nodded.

'You were all there?'

The men nodded again, all except Matty Bruton who quickly said, 'Not me.'

'All the rest of you were?'

Matt Dillon spoke for them. 'Yes.'

'Ten – twelve of you?'

'Yes.'

'And you're asking me believe that ten or twelve of you couldn't bring one sick man in without shooting him?'

They hadn't seen that coming.

'He had his gun on us when we went in,' Matt Dillon said, glancing about him for someone to corroborate his lie.

'That's just how it was,' Tom Bell agreed. 'It would have been him or some of us.'

'And you'll all swear to that, I suppose?'

'Sure we will. It's the truth.'

It wasn't, of course.

'You said they'd take him to hospital,' I accused Mam.

'I know, son. I'm sorry.'

'They never meant to let him get better.'

'Shush now.'

'It was awful, Mam.'

'I know. I know.'

'No you don't,' I said, and pulled away from Mam, almost making her topple. She looked at me as if I'd hit her. I'd never pulled away from Mam before, not when she was cuddling me and trying to comfort me. But now I was glad she felt hurt, and in the cruel way that children do I determined to make her suffer. 'I'll tell you what happened and then you *will* know,' I shouted, and was pleased as she put her hands to her face and looked stricken again. I told her everything, every detail, every horror.

All the men piled into the little pantry, pushing at each other to be the first to see.

'Shit Jesus,' Matt Dillon said.

'Christ!' said Tom Bell.

'God Almighty,' said Morrissey.

They were gawping at Kitty Daley. Her eyes had fallen in, and her open mouth was filled with thickish liquid that trickled down her chin. Something was going on inside her 'cause her skin was moving, a bit like she was having a slow shiver. Her flesh folded over the twine that bound her ankles making them big as a heifer's hocks.

'The bastard,' Matt Dillon breathed, and walked across the room, and kicked Dan. Kicked him hard in the stomach. Dan opened his eyes, blinked, and said, 'Hello,

Matt.' Matt kicked him again, furious. Then he grabbed Dan by the arm, almost wrenching it from the injured shoulder, and dragged him along the floor to the mattress. 'Look at her, you bastard,' he ordered. Dan kept his eyes closed.

'Look at her I said.'

Dan opened his eyes and looked. 'Kitty,' he said softly.

'Yeah, Kitty. Kitty Daley that was 'til you tortured her and killed her.'

Dan looked puzzled.

'And raped her more'n likely,' Morrissey said. And, watching, you could see the evilness creep into them all.

'Well if he wanted her that badly he can have her now,' Matt Dillon decided. 'Give us a hand.'

'Leave him alone,' I shouted.

'You stay out of this, boy,' Matt Dillon shouted.

'You leave him alone.'

'Don't mind the boy, Matt. Let's get on with it.'

Tom Bell took Dan's feet, and Matt Dillon his arms, and after swinging him a few times to gain height they dumped him on top of Kitty. Most of the other men roared their approval. It was like they were drunk. Their eyes gleamed, and they licked their lips, and they hopped about from foot to foot. But Frank Barnes went into the corner and waited.

'What's the matter with him?' Tom Bell asked, sneering.

'Squeamish. No stomach,' someone answered.

'Go on, Dan. You fuck her now,' someone yelled.

'Yeah. Go on, Dan. Go on, Dan,' they chorused. It was like the circus all over again.

Dan lay there, twitching, frightened and bewildered.

'Maybe he's forgot how,' Morrissey said.

'You goin' to show him how then?' someone shouted mockingly, and they all roared again.

Then they took to goading Morrissey: 'Yeah. You show him how, Morrissey.'

'Maybe you could teach us all a thing or two.'

'Keep braggin' about how sharp you are between the sheets. Now's your chance.'

'Got cold feet then?'

'No stomach, more like.'

Morrissey was getting into a terrible state. You could see him wondering how he'd got himself into such a mess, wondering how the hell he was going to get out of it.

And the men kept at him:

'Always sorts the men from the boys, making them act instead of talk.'

'That's for sure.'

'Thought you was a man, Morrissey.'

'Bet he's never even done it. Ever.'

'Yes I have,' Morrissey protested, the slur on his prowess more than he could stand.

'Well, give Dan a hand then.'

'Yeah. Go on. Help the poor bastard out.'

'Aw, shit. Damn well knew he knew nothing about it. Can't even show a fool how to do it.'

'Sure I'll show him how,' Morrissey said, and he jumped on to the mattress and sat astride Dan and started pumping up and down. He got off like a flash when Kitty's body seemed to collapse with a funny hissing, and white fluid splattered everywhere.

Dan looked up. Oddly, he was grinning, or seemed to be. The men thought he was, that's for sure, and it made them furious.

'Laughing at us, are you?' Matt Dillon screamed.

'That's what he's doing, Matt.'

'It's the last time he does it then,' Matt Dillon said. He pushed Dan with his boot, toppling him on to his back. Then he put his rifle right between Dan's eyes. Dan blinked and smiled again and looked quite pleased with the way things were going.

162

Matt Dillon fired his gun, and the next thing Dan was still lying on the mattress but his head was gone.

'I'm sorry. I'm sorry. I'm sorry,' Mam moaned.

I was sorry too. Sorry for Dan. Sorry for me. Sorry for Mam. Mostly for Mam, I think, since I knew she'd meant well. In a way I wasn't too sorry for Dan. He was happy now if all the things they told us were true. I wasn't too sorry for myself either since, to my way of thinking, Dan was all mine now.

27

The men got away with it, and it was better so, everyone agreed. Better for them certainly, and probably better for Dan in the long run.

And Matty Bruton got the farm and tore down the old farmhouse and built a fine new house in its place, one with big windows from which you could see the ocean, and he made a fortune renting it to folk from the city during the summer. He put caravans on the lower field, and made a fortune from that too.

And the men still gather in Biddlecombe's to chatter, but they don't seem to have that much to say to each other any more. It only takes a wrong word to make all of them edgy, look at one another suspicious, and drain their glasses, and leave.

Hey, Dan, I say. How are you? And I tell him what's going on, who got married, who died, who left and went to America or Australia or London. And I tell him what it's like in the woods, and about the foxes and birds. And I tell him how Mrs Biddlecombe slipped off her high chair and broke her hip, and how they gave her a new one in the city hospital, and how it's just as good as the old one, better since she can't break it. And I tell him how Matt Dillon's wife ran off and left him, ran off with someone half her age, a lad Matt brought from up the coast to help with the shearing. And I tell him that people are saying Matt Dillon's gone a bit soft in the head now, and won't come out much since people are laughing at him for losing his wife to a whippersnapper. And I tell him how Mrs Daley's doing nicely, and sporting fine new dresses since she got some sort of compensation.

I don't tell him what Matty Bruton's done to the farm though. He wouldn't like that.

It's nice to have Dan to talk to. Mam and I don't have much to say to each other now. And I don't speak to God any more.